Alfred Aspland

Triumph of the Emperor Maximilian I

Anatiposi

Alfred Aspland

Triumph of the Emperor Maximilian I

Reprint of the original, first published in 1875.

1st Edition 2024 | ISBN: 978-3-38282-853-0

Anatiposi Verlag is an imprint of Outlook Verlagsgesellschaft mbH.

Verlag (Publisher): Outlook Verlag GmbH, Zeilweg 44, 60439 Frankfurt, Deutschland
Vertretungsberechtigt (Authorized to represent): E. Roepke, Zeilweg 44, 60439 Frankfurt, Deutschland
Druck (Print): Books on Demand GmbH, In de Tarpen 42, 22848 Norderstedt, Deutschland

TRIUMPH

OF THE

EMPEROR MAXIMILIAN I.

THE HOLBEIN SOCIETY'S FAC-SIMILE REPRINTS.

TRIUMPH

OF THE EMPEROR

MAXIMILIAN I.

WITH WOODCUTS

Designed by HANS BURGMAIR.

EDITED BY

ALFRED ASPLAND, F. R. Hist. S.

Reproduced by the HOLBEIN SOCIETY.

1875.

TABLE OF CONTENTS.

ERRATA.

—

At Page 64, line 9, *for* "mazes" *read* "majesty."

At Page 162, line 4, a *t* reversed.

THE Emperor Maximilian I. was born A.D. 1459, and succeeded to the throne of his ancestors in 1493 as head of the Holy Roman Empire. His father, Frederick III., weak, incapable, and treacherous, transmitted to his son an impoverished, degraded, and dismembered empire. Frederick was the last of the Emperors crowned at Rome; and although he commenced his reign by summoning the Council of Basle, which proposed reforms in the Church, the emissaries of Rome having persuaded him that his interests lay in an opposite direction, he deserted the Council, and took sides with the Pope. It happened thus,—being a trifler in literature, he was charmed with the elegant poetry and free novels of the secretary to the Council, Pius Æneas Silvius Piccolomini, and he placed on the brows of this adventurer, with much solemnity and ceremonial, the poet's wreath. The Emperor returned home, and was followed by Silvius, who was deputed by the Council to confer with him on the projected reforms. He transferred his services from the Council to the Empire, and Frederick, having made him his private secretary, sent him to Rome to urge the Pope to submit to the Diet.

His versatile talents and capacity for intrigue being at once recognized, he was induced to desert the Emperor and become an ecclesiastic. He addressed himself to Caspar Schlick, the imperial chancellor. Frederick, now as ever the tool of others, was persuaded to oppose the Diet and stifle the reforms projected by the Council. He concluded a concordat with Nicholas V., which rendered him despised and hated by the opponents of Rome. The art of printing coming into use about this time, rendered the art of reigning more difficult, especially to a monarch like Frederick, deficient in money and troops. To strengthen his position, he looked abroad among the European Houses for a suitable bride, and in 1452 he married Eleonora of

B

Portugal, who had beauty, spirit, and wit. The wedding festivities were conducted at Naples with great magnificence. The wedded pair proceeded to Rome, and were crowned. The Empress had not long to wait to see the character of her husband. Whilst all Europe was convulsed with war, and chivalric monarchs were heading their troops in the field, he was content to shut himself up in his castle, cultivating his garden, and, engaging in other trifles, left his chancellor Caspar to extricate him from the network of troubles in which he was politically entangled. Had he been able to read the signs of the times, or had he even adhered to his pledges, Luther's mission might not have been required, and a safe and quiet reformation might · have been effected. Had he evinced any manly courage, the nobles of the Empire, instead of treating him with insolent contempt, would have rallied round him, and prevented province after province being torn from the Empire. An electoral assembly met to depose him, but came to no decision, owing to the prevailing confusion, and was unnoticed by him. Vienna revolted, and refused him admission to his own castle. He suffered the greatest indignities, and condescended to flatter his rebellious subjects. He was admitted at last, and his indignant empress said aloud to her son Maximilian, " Could I believe you capable of demeaning yourself like your father, I should lament your being destined to the throne " (A.D. 1463). Austria had now become a den of lawless robbers, who carried their audacity to such a height as to rob the Empress whilst taking the waters of Baden. The aid of Matthias of Hungary was called in, and many hundreds of the rovers were hanged or drowned. In the midst of all these troubles Frederick the Emperor made a pilgrimage to Rome, in performance of a pious vow. He left a body of unpaid mercenaries, who on his return were clamorous and threatening. He might have paid them in the false coinage which he had ordered to be struck ; he simply refused to pay, whereupon one of his most faithful adherents, Andreas Baumkirchner, volunteered to be their advocate. Frederick met him at Grätz, and promised him safety till vespers. He detained him till the close of day, and then caused him to be murdered as he was passing out of the gate.

We now approach a period of greater interest in the history of this infamous emperor. His son Maximilian had attained manhood, and Frederick made proposals on his behalf for the hand of Mary, daughter of Charles the Bold, Duke of Burgundy. At this time Louis XI. was pursuing the heiress of Burgundy for his son, the Dauphin, a boy of seven years of age.

The Count of Angoulême, a prince of the blood-royal of France, was a third candidate. His pretensions were set aside by the intrigues of Louis. Charles favoured the young Archduke of Austria, and he and Frederick met at Trèves (A.D. 1473). Charles claimed from the Emperor the title of King of Burgundy. Frederick, not unwilling to comply, but for once in his life determined not to be a dupe, insisted on the immediate conclusion of the marriage before the title was granted. To this Charles demurred, and procrastinated the negotiations. The Emperor withdrew suddenly, without the courtesy of a leave-taking. The Pope, notwithstanding the Emperor's subserviency, sided with Charles, and the negotiations were at an end.

Philip de Commines tells us that whilst the marriage of the Princess Mary with the Dauphin was under consideration, Madam Hallewin, first lady of the bedchamber to that princess, gave it as her opinion " that there was more need of a man than a boy."

The meaning of this saying, and the magnitude of the prize, will be understood when we remember that Mary was sole heiress not only of the duchy of Burgundy, but of Franche-Comté, Artois, Flanders, and of almost all the Netherlands.

Burgundy remained a duchy, and the bold and restless duke fell fighting before Nancy in 1477. Louis XI. claimed the duchy of Burgundy as a male fief, and the guardianship of Mary. In relation to this juncture of affairs, Menzel, in his History of Germany, says,--" Mary of Burgundy, anxious alike to escape the merciless grasp of this royal monster (Louis XI.) and the rule of the wild democracy of

Ghent, at first endeavoured to conciliate the Dutch by the promulgation of the great Charter, in which she vowed, neither to marry nor to levy taxes, nor to make war without their consent, and conceded to them the right of convoking the Estates, of minting, and of freely voting on every question. In the hope of gaining a greater accession of power by a foreign marriage, she skilfully worked upon the dread with which the French were viewed by her subjects, to influence them in favour of Maximilian, the handsomest youth of his day, whom she is said to have seen at an earlier period at Trèves, or, as some say, of whose picture she had become, enamoured. Maximilian inherited the physical strength of his grandmother, Cimburga of Poland, and the mental qualities of his Portuguese mother; surpassed all other knights in chivalric feats ; was modest, gentle, and amiable. Mary confessed to the assembled Estates of the Netherlands that she had already interchanged letters and rings with him, and the marriage was resolved upon. Maximilian hastened to Ghent, and, mounted on a brown steed, clothed in silver-gilt armour, his long blond locks crowned with a bridegroom's wreath, resplendent with pearls and precious stones, rode into the city, where he was met by Mary. The youthful pair, on beholding one another, knelt in the public street and sank into each other's arms. ‘Welcome art thou to me,’ thou noble German,’ said the young duchess, ‘whom I have so long desired and now behold with delight !’ ” *

This melodramatic scene is hardly consistent with the maiden modesty of the lady, or with the impulsive and chivalric character of the young archduke, who would be naturally the first to express the ardour of his affection. Wolfgang Menzel, though highly esteemed as a German author, is not unfrequently inaccurate. There are two reasons why we should doubt the story : Philip de Commines, who gives in his Memoirs thirty-four years of the reign of Louis XI. and Charles VIII., his successor, distinctly states

* Menzel's "History of Germany," translated by Mrs. George Horrocks from the fourth German edition. Bell & Daldy. London, 1871-2.

that Mary had favoured the suit of the Count of Angou-
lesme. (Mem., vol. vi. chap. iii.) Next, in the autobiography
of Maximilian, prefacing the woodcuts illustrating Der Weis
Kunig (the Wise King), a history is given of the meeting
with Mary, but nothing like the above is related. It will
be given further on.

Maximilian, immediately on his marriage, devoted himself to improving the internal government of Austria,
which the indolence of his father had allowed to drift into
utter confusion. He, although not possessed of the highest
powers of statesmanship, was incomparably the best and
most accomplished prince which the House of Hapsburg
has produced; he had energy, and a strong desire to re-
form abuses; and had not much of his time been occupied
in fighting, and if he could have commanded money and
troops, he would undoubtedly have accomplished his projected plans.

In his and his father's reign the four great events of the
fifteenth century occurred,—the dawn of the Reformation,
the discovery of America by Columbus (1492), the destruction of the Greek empire by Sultan Mahommed III. (1453),
the invention of printing (1457); and yet neither father nor
son in any way recognized the portentous results that would
ensue from these events. Maximilian was highly educated,
and if we accept his own version of his studies and their
results, his knowledge was encyclopedic. We distinguish
two sides in his character, the practical and the romantic.
He illustrated the former aspect by his attention to mechanical inventions and domestic arrangements. He
planned out the division of Germany into circles, to insure
some order and regularity in the government, and to pro-
vide for the better administration of justice, superseding
by degrees the Vehm Courts,* which were unsuited to the
spirit of the age.

The romantic aspect of his character is indicated by his
poetry, his love of tilts, tournays, feats of arms, and chal-
lenge of dangers. He was, indeed, a connecting link be-

---

* See Appendix.

tween mediæval chivalry and modern prosaic life. And
this chivalric disposition might have brightened into a truly
chivalric life, with its self-denials and worship of personal
honour ; but the times were against him ; the Holy Roman
Empire was becoming a sham ; a Borgia was on the throne
of St. Peter ; amongst princes, treachery and dissimulation
were the rule in diplomatic intercourse, and he had to face
internal dissensions and aggression from without, circumstances little favourable to the development of a noble
life. His domestic relations were troubled. He early
lost his beautiful wife, Mary of Burgundy, whom he
tenderly loved, and who would have ennobled his policy
and strengthened his good intentions. She certainly would
have saved him from the ill-will and revolt of his Flemish
subjects, who never recognized his authority except as the
guardian of his son Philip. His nobleness of mien, his
gallantry and affability, endeared him to his people, but
brought him no favour from the princes of the Empire,
who constantly thwarted all his projects relating to war
and finance. It was his misfortune to follow a weak
driveller like Frederick III., who created a turbulent
opposition to his illustrious house.

The House of Hapsburg, destined to occupy the throne
of Austria for nearly six centuries, was founded by a
robber knight, whose castle of Hapsburg stood on a lofty
eminence on the right bank of the Aar, in the canton of
Ber, in the Helvetic republic. Nearly a century had elapsed
since the death of Frederick Barbarossa, of Hohenstaufen,
the last of that race capable of asserting the supremacy of
the Empire over the Papacy. After him his feeble de-
scendants for awhile held the imperial sceptre without
imperial power. At last came an interregnum, owing to
the squabbles of the Electors, who would have sold the
Empire to the highest bidder. It was now without a head,
and absolute anarchy prevailed. The Pope, finding his
revenues declining and his power lessening, threatened the
Electors that he would appoint an emperor if they omitted
their duty. They selected Rudolph on account of his insig-
nificance. The Pope crowned him at Lausanne, to give him

no pretence to go to Rome, and made it a condition of his support that he should overthrow Ottocar, king of Bohemia. This he accomplished, and then devoted himself to the aggrandisement of his family by marriages and intrigues. Bold and fearless as the class from which he sprung usually were, and liking the excitement of fighting, he undertook work degrading enough to a monarch of such rank as the Roman Empire brought, and suitable for a subaltern rather than for an emperor; and so we find him putting down petty feuds, and fighting with robbers. He showed no affection for those who followed his former trade, but amused himself (after having been beaten by the Bernese in a great battle) in destroying robber castles. Sixty-six fell under his assaults, and he hanged twenty-nine of the robber knights at Ilmenan. In his old age he married Agnes of Burgundy, a girl in her fourteenth year. It is related that the Bishop of Spires was so enchanted with her beauty, that after the ceremony he kissed her, and the Emperor suggested to the Bishop that it was the Agnus Dei, not Agnes, that he ought to kiss. The whilome freebooter died in his bed in 1292. Such was the founder of the House of Hapsburg. Dante in his " Purgatorio " gives a place to Rudolph :—

> " May on thy race Heaven's just judgment fall ;
> And be it signally and plainly shown,
> With terror thy successor to appal,
> Since by thy lust yon distant lands to gain,
> Thou and thy sire * have suffered wild to run
> What was the garden of the fair domain."
>
> Canto VI. l. 101.†

The theory of the Holy Roman Empire. Jurists have generally agreed that it meant Church and State in their closest relationship, both deriving their authority from God, the Papacy being the spiritual member, the Empire the temporal, neither perfect without the other. The Pope

---

* Rudolf I.
† Translation by J. C. Wright, M.A. Bohn. London, 1854.

was to depend on the Emperor to protect him and the faith, as his kingdom was not of this world ; the Emperor was to be earthly lord of this world, and to wield the sword to compel obedience to the decrees of the Church.

The Papacy has held various views ; at one time owning subjection to the Empire, as when Leo III. crowned Charlemagne, and worshipped him. Hildebrand (Gregory VII.) claimed absolute power, both temporal and spiritual, power to depose or institute princes of the earth ; and, acting on this, passed sentence of excommunication on the Emperor Henry IV.

The Imperial view of the relations of the State and the Church was as various as that of the Papacy. Charlemagne looked upon the Emperor as head of the State and Church, as himself the Pope, the occupier of St. Peter's throne as only his instrument and subject.

The whole of the imperial life of Frederick I. (Barbarossa) was devoted to the depression of the Papal power. On his arrival at Rome to be crowned by the Pope, his indignation was roused at seeing a picture publicly exposed in the Lateran, representing Lothair's acceptance of the crown in fee from the Pope. He ordered it to be removed (some say burnt), and used these threatening words :—"God has raised the Church by means of the State, the Church, nevertheless, will overthrow the State. She has commenced by painting, and from painting has proceeded to writing. Writing will gain the mastery over all, if we permit it. Efface your pictures, and remove your documents, that peace may be preserved between the State and the Church." Rogers ("Italy"), in describing St. Mark's Place, sings :—

> "In that temple porch
> (The brass is gone, the porphyry remains)
> Did Barbarossa fling his mantle off,
> And, kneeling, on his neck received the foot
> Of the proud Pontiff."

This legend, like a thousand others about the great Emperor, is probably as true as that he and his knights are now in a cave almost inaccessible to human foot, resting in an enchanted sleep, waiting till the world again wants a hero to avenge its wrongs.

Frederick III., the father of Maximilian, looked upon the Empire as the tool and slave of the Papacy, as witnessed by his abject submission and superstitious reverence.

Dante (*De Monarchia*) held that Emperor and Pope both derive their power from God ; that Leo acted wrongfully in bestowing the Empire on Charlemagne : that Constantine's Donation was illegal ;* that no single emperor or pope can destroy the everlasting foundation of their thrones. " Two guides are needed, the Pontiff and the Emperor, the latter of whom, in order that he may direct mankind in accordance with the teachings of philosophy to temporal blessedness, must preserve universal peace in the world. Thus are the two powers equally ordained of God, and the Emperor, though supreme in all that pertains to the secular world, is in some things dependent on the Pontiff, since earthly happiness is subordinate to eternal. Let Cæsar, therefore, show towards Peter the reverence wherewith a first-born son honours his father, that, being illumined by the light of his paternal favour, he may the more excellently shine forth upon the whole world, to the rule of which he has been appointed by Him alone who is of all things, both spiritual and temporal, the King and Governor ! So ends the treatise." †

Whatever the theories may have been, the practical results were for centuries conflicts for supremacy, intrigues, and bloody wars. Dante's theory, if carried out, would have stopped all human progress, by fettering the minds and enslaving the bodies of the human race within the range of Christendom. What the Holy Roman Empire was in later years is pithily put by Voltaire,—it was not Holy, it was not Roman, and in no reasonable sense Imperial.

In the year 800, Charlemagne entered Rome, and heard mass in St. Peter's on Christmas eve. Whilst kneeling at the high altar, attired in the sandals and chlamys of a

---

* Dante did not know that it was a forgery.   † Dr. Bryce.

Roman patrician, the Pope, Leo III., rose from his throne
and placed the imperial crown on the brows of the victorious Frankish king.   He then bent in obeisance before
him, and the Holy Roman Empire was established.*

We pass on to a period, embracing 693 years, during
which, with various fortunes, forty-five princes were established on the imperial throne, now rising to the grandeur
and power of Barbarossa, now reigning as mere tools of
the electors and popes ; at one time the title blotted out
and an interregnum of nearly twenty years occurring.   In
1493, Maximilian ascended the throne, and with him died
in fact the Holy Roman Empire.   Neither he nor any
succeeding emperor was crowned at Rome, and though the
German emperors after this date assumed on their coins the
titular sovereignty of Rome, it was for the future a vanity,
and a delusion.   Maximilian took his title Emperor-elect
with the consent of the Pope,† but as he was not crowned
at Rome, nor even by the Pope himself, his real rank was
simply German Emperor ; he was not recognized as head
of Christendom, and though his pompous titles gratified
his vanity, they merely represented traditions.   With
Maximilian began the entire severance of Germany from
Rome, and, as no subsequent emperor was crowned at
Rome by the Pope, the term Holy Roman Empire ceased
to have meaning.   Maximilian did attempt to go to
Rome and receive the crown imperial at St. Peter's : his
humiliating defeat and its results will be described in the
narrative of his battles (page 21).   That he would have been
an unwelcome guest at Rome is probable enough, as he had
in 1500 issued a decree that two-thirds of the sums gained
by the sale of indulgences should be retained in the
Empire, and applied to its defence against the Turks ;
later on he suggested that the different relations of the
Empire and the Papacy should be settled by his own
assumption of both offices, but his decree was disregarded

---

* "The Holy Roman Empire." By James Bryce, D.C.L., Regius Professor of Civil Law in the University of Oxford.   Fourth edition.   MacMillan
& Co. London, 1873.   † See Appendix.

by his own subjects, and the cardinals managed to prevent his spiritual pretensions being realized. The Holy Roman Empire was recognized in treaties till 1648, when both Catholic and Protestant princes extorted from Ferdinand III. full recognition of their sovereignty, independently of his authority, and Lutherans and Calvinists were declared free from all jurisdiction of the Pope and all Catholic prelates. This was the upshot of the Thirty Years' War, ending with the peace of Westphalia.. The Empire existed in name till the year 1806, when Francis II. resigned the crown, and bore to the end of his life, and transmitted to his successors, the title of Emperor of Austria. And now, in the year 1874, we find Catholic Austria defying the Pope, and the Emperor declining the courtesy of an answer to Pius IX. But there is a new German Empire which utterly ignores the Pope, and at present is depriving and imprisoning Catholic archbishops and bishops for obeying his Encyclical.

(*Reuter's Telegrams.*)

A NEW ENCYCLICAL.

" VIENNA, *Saturday, March* 7.

"An encyclical letter of the Pope, addressed to the Austrian bishops, and dated 7th inst., has been published. The Pope condemns the ecclesiastical bills submitted by the Austrian Government to the Reichsrath, and declares that their object is to bring the Roman Catholic Church into most ruinous subjection to the arbitrary power of the State. His Holiness admits that the Austrian laws appear moderate as compared with those enacted by Prussia ; nevertheless, they are of the same spirit and character, and pave the way for the same destruction of the Church in Austria as in Prussia. The Pope renews his protest against the rupture of the Concordat, and describes the assertion that a change was brought about in the Church by the dogma of infallibility as a pernicious pretext, and hopes that the bishops will protect the rights of the Church. His Holiness at the same time announces that in a fresh letter to the Emperor Francis Joseph, dated the 7th inst., he adjured his Majesty not to allow the Church to be handed over to dishonourable servitude, and his Catholic subjects to be visited by the deepest affliction."

And notwithstanding this almost abject appeal, we read further, March 14, " The Lower House of the Reichsrath continued the debate on the first ecclesiastical bill to-day. The bill was read a second time in the form in which it was brought forward by the committee, and a resolution was added in favour of separating the parishes in Austrian territory from the diocese of Breslau." This hostile proceeding is thus explained :—

(*Reuter's Telegrams.*)

" VIENNA, *Tuesday, March* 17, 1874.

"It is stated that the Emperor does not intend to give explanations to the Roman Curia respecting the Austrian ecclesiastical laws. The Pope's letter to the Emperor Francis Joseph has been handed by his Majesty to the Minister for Foreign Affairs."

We take leave of the Holy Roman Empire and turn to consider one of the causes of its decay and dissolution,— the Renaissance, which defies definition, as it had, besides its classical and pagan tendencies, its scientific, religious, and christian developments. It is interesting to watch its progress as a revolt against authority, as a determination to assert the right to freedom of thought, and to explore the fertile sources of human culture.

As long as authority defines the mode of life of individuals, and is accepted as the true mode, national life is stationary, and progress is impossible. It matters not from what source authority springs, or how it is developed, the result is the same. It may be a national confederacy, as in India, defining the life, social and spiritual, or the theocratic rule as assumed by the ancient Jews, or its modern counterpart, government by a Church, whether it be East or West. As long as the nations implicitly believe in and accept it, the imaginative element is subdued, national life is saddened, and centuries may glide by before happier influences prevail. The natural mutability of human affairs comes at last to the rescue. Passionate impulses towards things of beauty have no doubt existed in all ages, and genius necessarily derides the control of authority and convention. Where the passionate impulse becomes a national trait, authority is defied, and national life changes its aspect. So it was with the Renaissance. During the Middle Ages its progress was slow, but it existed, giving a faint and partial colouring of beauty to men's lives. It worked individually, and by fits and starts. In the eleventh century, we find Abelard, the famous clerk, and his no less famous mistress, Heloise, mastering the difficulties of philosophy and scholarship, he at the same time writing his love songs, which the youth of France chanted in the streets. Next we have the Trouvères, or Jongleurs, spreading over France and Italy, singing of chivalry, and love, and the mighty deeds of crusading knights, contributing their part to this many-sided movement, — the Renaissance. Its blooming-time was Italy in the fifteenth century, and part of the sixteenth, when classical literature and pagan art so completely entranced the minds of the Italian poets, that theology, philosophy, and medicine, indeed all literature, was Olympian in its taste and feeling. Poetic fancy recognized and described Christ as one of the Homeric heroes, and the Virgin is found by the angel Gabriel reading the books of the Sibyls, instead of the Psalms. Patristic literature was thrown aside for the works of Plato and Aristotle, Homer and Virgil were substituted for the Missal, and authors deriding the barbarous Latin of the dark ages, vied with each other in classical purity of style. Ecclesiasticism was opposed by reason, and spiritual writers branched off in two directions, one, in the attempt to reconcile christianity with paganism ; the other, in opposing authority, and demanding the right to personal free inquiry, to enjoy its results, and so to enable men to live a truly religious life, in conformity with their inmost convictions.

In art, Renaissance audacity was equally remarkable; instead of Pietas, of portraits of saints, martyrs, and of Our Lady, and pictures of the tragedy of Calvary, painters revelled in the nude, and gave sensuous expression to the pagan deities.

Science marched with equal strides, and under the patronage and support of the illustrious house of the Medici, and some of the popes, the ages of slumber and darkness were looked upon as barbarous, and men became too busy with their new-found treasures to take any interest in the squabbles of Popes and Emperors. A few examples will illustrate these remarks.

Angelus Politianus was born in Tuscany, A.D. 1454. As a mere child, the dawnings of his genius were watched with interest by Lorenzo de' Medici, who furnished the means for his education, and when this was completed, he was called to be the tutor of his patron's children. He soon was recognized as the most distinguished scholar in Italy, and students of the greatest distinction from all parts of Europe began to resort to Florence, to benefit by his instructions. He was thoroughly imbued with the Greek spirit. His poetry excited the greatest enthusiasm. It was chiefly composed for academic purposes, and read before he commenced his lectures. His theme was the ancient classic author whose works he was about to criticise. He translated Homer after he was made a canon of Florence, and was a well-known writer of Greek poetry. Tiraboschi, in his *Storia della Poesia Italiana*, speaking of Politian as one of the purifiers of the Italian language, says: "It is a matter of real astonishment that at a time when those who had been longest exercised in the practice of versification could not divest themselves of their antiquated rusticity, a youthful poet, who had scarce begun to touch the lyre, should be able to leave them so far behind." Richardson, in his book upon painting, says that the influence which Politian exercised over Raffaelle was most distinct. The charges against him of infidelity and licentiousness of life have been clearly disproved. The exuberance of youth and poetic ecstasy led him occasionally into some indiscretions of language,—that is all that can be said against him. In the execution of his ecclesiastical duties, he read and expounded the Bible to the people, and yet a modern author, Abbé Gaume, in his *Ver Rongeur des Sociétés Modernes*, thus sums up his character:—"He esteemed and taught nothing during the whole course of life but pure paganism. He wrote in Italian verse lewd songs and tragedies entirely in the pagan taste, and these were elegantly printed at Florence." He died at the age of forty-one. By his express desire to the attendants of his death-bed, his remains were invested in the habit of the Dominicans.

His intimate friend and frequent companion, Picus of Mirandula, Prince of Mirandula, was born A.D. 1463, died 1494. His genius and erudition, his early ambition to distinguish himself publicly by offering to defend nine hundred paradoxes, drawn from the most opposite sources, against all comers; his remarkable beauty, and his extensive charities, attracted the gaze of Italy. He wrote love songs, which in a fervour of piety he burnt. He studied paganism with an eager desire to reconcile it with Christianity—"to bind the ages each to each with natural piety."

Sannazarius, perhaps more than any Italian poet, wrapt himself up in the classical mantle. He was born at Naples, 1458, died 1530, and was celebrated as a scholar and poet. Ferdinand, king of Naples, invited him to his court, and he became the intimate associate of his son Frederick. He wrote a poem, *De Partu Virginis*, which was carried out with the agency of Dryads and Nereids, the books of the Sibyls substituted for those of the Prophets; and Proteus is represented as predicting the mystery of the Incarnation. His tomb is an object of curiosity even now, at Posilipo, at a villa which during his lifetime Sannazarius had converted into a church, dedicated to the Virgin Mother and St. Nazaro.* "Behind the high altar rises the mausoleum of the poet, formed of Parian marble, the top a half-length likeness of him, crowned with a leaf of laurel; beneath, stand on the right and left two marble statues of Minerva and Apollo, while Satyrs are seen sporting in the middle." Modern propriety has re-christened them David and Judith.

This selection from a long list of Renaissance writers will suffice; the other poets necessary for a sketch appear as painters.

The eleventh century found art in its lowest state of

* Rev. W. Parr Cresswell, "Memoirs of Politian," &c. Cadell & Davis. London, 1805.

degradation : bloody martyrdoms, and Christ in his utmost suffering, were the favourite subjects of the artists.

The Council of Constantinople had three centuries before taken off the interdict against painting the figure of Christ, but as the Church dominated all art, and that of Byzantium had no touch of nature in it, and was conventionally grotesque and stationary, as the work of ascetic monks in their cells must be, we find a constant repetition of emaciated Christs with dull staring eyes, gloomy Madonnas and repulsive saints. The object being, not art, but the representation of the religious life, necessarily rendered artists afraid of incurring the censure of the Church if they disturbed the conventional style. And so matters went on till the thirteenth century, when we witness signs of the Renaissance in the work of Nicolas Pisano, who in his paintings gave the first indications of form, and a knowledge of what the Greeks had accomplished.

Giotto (born 1276, died 1336) boldly threw aside Byzantine traditions, and copied nature with true artistic feeling. He indicated religious life as known to the Franciscans, to which order he belonged. The bell-tower of S. Maria del Fiore, which the modern traveller sees with delight, was the last work of Giotto in Florence, showing that, like other great painters, he could excel in architecture. Dante loved him, and in his *Purgatorio* describes how he eclipsed Cimabue.

A century and a quarter roll on, and science is making rapid strides ; works on mathematics and perspective appear, and Masacchio's (born 1402, died 1428) paintings exhibit the deepening influence. " The spirit of classical antiquity," says Mrs. Heaton, " lives again, in fact, in his works, but the spirit of Christianity is fast dying out." *

A few years more, and art attains its meridian. Leonardo da Vinci, Michelangelo, and Raffaelle have appeared and done their work. As to the two first, although doubtless influenced by all that had preceded and was around them,

---

* " A Concise History of Painting." By Mrs. Charles Heaton. Bell & Daldy, 1873.

there are traces of mediævalism, and anticipations of the future, which render their exact position as regards the Renaissance a very complex problem. Though painting christian pictures, the hold of the Church upon them is gone. In Raffaelle, the Greek spirit bursts forth with uncontrolled energy, and when not engaged on christian art, he revels in Olympus, and gods and goddesses appear in as sensuous forms as the refined and æsthetic mind of Raffaelle could permit. His joyous life and early death, in strong contrast with the long sad life, the austerity of manner, and the deep under current of tenderness of Michelangelo, are stories too well known to need repeating here.

The Renaissance in Germany worked altogether in a different direction from the revival in Italy. In the latter country pagan learning and art led men away from faith and dogmas and scholastic theology. Martin Luther relates with what holy joy he first entered Rome, and with what devoutness he said masses daily, even wishing that his father and mother were dead, that he might save their souls from purgatory ; and how he found he was derided by the priests, who thought him absurdly credulous; and how, when he was in the society of prelates, he found that they joined in the impious chorus. One related as a good joke, that in the Sacrament of the Eucharist, instead of the prescribed formula, he muttered, " Panis es et panis manebis, vinum es et vinum manebis,"—" Bread thou art and bread thou wilt remain, wine thou art and wine thou wilt remain." Macchiavelli said that "we Italians are in-debted to the Church and the priests for our having become a set of complete scoundrels."

Luther returned, brooding over these things ; and the great monk saw the reformation which he believed he had a divine call to accomplish.

In early life his study of the Greek sophists occupied his whole attention. He says, in his Table-talk, " When I was young, then I was learned, and especially before I came into divinity, then I dealt altogether with allegories, tropoligies, anagogies ; there was nothing about me but altogether art ; but I knew it was not worth a sir-reverence ;

D

now I have shaken it off, and my best art is to deliver the Scripture in the simple sense; the same doth the deed, therein is life, strength, doctrine, and art; in the other is nothing but foolishness, let it shine how it will. When men will aim at that scope and make tropes, then we that are Christians have lost."

Although Luther was a scholar, he seems to have turned from Greek authors, and confined his reading to the Roman writers. Reuchlin, Melancthon, Erasmus, and the mass of German scholars of that day avoided the pagan spirit which Italy affected, and went in the direction of faith, and under their teaching and writings the breach between Rome and Germany widened apace. The final triumph of the Reformers was only the completion of what had been going on in Maximilian's time, and the right of private judgment which they whimsically assumed as the basis of the Reformation, weakened the hold of the Emperor upon the obedience of every individual in his empire.

Other matters of importance were separating the Empire from the Church. The Pope entered into a league with France against Maximilian, and he in his turn proposed, nay issued, a decree to intercept a portion of the Papal revenue. He received no money, and exasperated both the Papacy and the Reformers. He afterwards intrigued for the Papacy.

To understand the engravings which Burgmair designed for his Triumph, we must trace the general outlines of his history, and note his family alliances and his wars.

The chivalric young prince had just married Mary of Burgundy, and her large dowry, for the first time in his life, placed him beyond the reach of poverty. Louis XI., on the death of the Duke of Burgundy, had seized the duchy of Burgundy, and occupied part of it. The Swiss, then occupying a portion, held him in restraint, and he was rejected by the Flemings. Maximilian drove the French king from the Netherlands, and in revenge, Louis then induced a faction of the Hoecks to take up arms against the Kabeljans. The Archduke favoured the cause of the latter, and, heading a body of mercenaries, bore all before him, gave his troops free license to murder and pillage, and executed the heads of the faction at Leyden (1479). Nearly three years of comparative peace gave Maximilian an opportunity of enjoying domestic happiness, and revolving in his mind those reforms which he afterwards carried out, or attempted to accomplish.

These were, the establishment of a Public Peace, the division of Germany into circles, the formation of an Aulic and Imperial Chamber, and the establishment of a Post-office. Menzel says they all fell through, and that he only rendered confusion systematic; but as Menzel was clearly prejudiced against Maximilian, and as indications of partial success are gleaned from many writers, we may more safely disregard his depreciation of Maximilian's character, and believe that a man who could plan such extensive reforms must have been possessed of considerable administrative ability. Confusion reigned everywhere; Alexander VI. occupied St. Peter's throne; Louis XI. was king of France; kings and princes were merely robbers of more or less magnitude; the Swiss, in spite of much patriotic feeling, were, when out of their own country, perfidious and mercenary bands, ready to sell their swords to the highest bidder, and to desert any cause for a bribe. Maximilian failed to establish on a safe basis a Roman empire, but he certainly laid a foundation for a safer establishment of the Hapsburg dynasty in Austria.

The establishment of the Germanic circles was intended to supersede the secret Vehme Gericht courts by the institution of open courts with known judges. (See Appendix.)

The imperial post-office was necessarily an imperfect development in the absence of roads, in the presence of robbers, and during the existence of wars.

In finance Maximilian's ill success was simply the result of his subjects' refusal to pay the common penny grant, an annual penny for every thousand possessed by a freeman, and of his incapacity to compel the payment.

However, whilst these plans were occupying the Emperor's attention, he had the misfortune to lose his wife, who died a few days after a fall from her horse in 1482. The Burgundians and Mary's subjects in the Netherlands, never well affected towards Maximilian, now rose in general revolt. The position was critical, and peace with France was necessary. The treaty of Arras settled this. The Emperor was to give his daughter Margaret in marriage to the Dauphin, with Boulogne and the county of Burgundy in dower, and Artois was to be restored to the Emperor. The young child Margaret was sent to Paris, and the lands given in dower were annexed to France. Philip de Commines, who is a better authority than Menzel, says that during the negotiations for this marriage the archduke was created king of the Romans. At peace with France, Maximilian marched at the head of all the forces he could collect, dislodged the Hoecks from Utrecht, and restored order; but the Flemings were still unwilling to submit to German rule. They managed to secure the person of Mary's son Philip, whom they looked upon as their ruler. The citizens of Bruges rose, and made Maximilian and his suite prisoners. The latter were tortured, and on the rumour of an approaching force sent by the Emperor Frederick, beheaded. Maximilian was imprisoned in a castle surrounded by a fosse, and the King's celebrated jester, Von Rosen, swam the fosse at night to rescue his master. He was baffled by the swans, which attacked him furiously, and drove him back (A.D. 1488).

The princes of the Empire rallied round the Emperor, and marched on Bruges, and the Pope excommunicated the rebels. The citizens were beaten, but not so that they were unable to make terms with Maximilian. He was obliged to take an oath not to revenge the wrongs done to his councillors and to himself. He had been imprisoned four months, and on his liberation retired to the Tyrol. He was beloved by the Tyrolese, and he returned their affection.

The imperial forces were successful, and there seemed a chance of peace, when Charles of France seized Anna, princess of Brittany, on her way to marry Maximilian, when the revolt in Flanders became general. Charles forced Anna to marry him, and having his eyes upon Italy, withdrew his troops from the Netherlands, and, unaided by foreign soldiers, the country was reduced to submission, and peace was concluded at Senlis (A D. 1493). A severe example was made of the citizens of Bruges ; forty of the most important were executed.

Margaret was returned to her father, Albert of Saxony restoring her and her brother Philip into the hands of Maximilian.

We have anticipated some events which concerned Maximilian. In 1482 an alliance between the Emperor and Wladislaw of Bohemia was concluded, and they marched against their common foe, Matthias of Hungary. Maximilian would, in all probability, lead his troops. They defeated Matthias near Bruck, on the Leytra. And we find him again, in 1487, defeating the Hungarians with superior forces at Negau. In 1490 Matthias of Hungary died. Maximilian stormed Vienna, and was wounded in the shoulder. He now led his troops into the centre of Hungary ; but his mercenaries collected so much plunder that they deserted their commander, and the campaign ended.

We return to the year 1493 :—Maximilian was robbed of his wife, his daughter was insultingly returned to him, Frederick his father died, and he became Emperor-Elect.

Owing to his poverty he was unable to lead the small body of men (3,000) he could send to the allied forces of the Pope, Spain, Naples, and the Turks,—against the most Christian king of France, meditating the annexation of Italy. The French king retired, and Maximilian vainly put forth some claims of his own. In 1496 he headed a small force in aid of Pisa, fighting against Florence. He was unsuccessful. He two years before this time had married Bianca Sforza, daughter of the duke of Milan. She had no personal charms ; her temper was cold, haughty, and imperious, and as the Emperor's object was simply political in contracting this alliance, it was, as might be expected, unhappy.

In 1496 Maximilian's son Philip and his daughter Margaret entered into important alliances with Spain, Philip marrying the Infanta, and Margaret marrying the Infant Don Juan. The Infant died shortly after, and Philip claimed the succession to Spain.

Troubles in Switzerland now began. The Switzers were determined to dissever their country from the Empire. In 1498 the Emperor declared war, and his confederates were beaten in every engagement. Still the Emperor persevered, and despatching a large body of troops under Count von Furstenberg, a decisive battle was fought near Dornach. The count was killed and his troops routed. Switzerland was free.

About this time disturbances occurred in the Netherlands, the inhabitants sustaining the claim of Charles of Gueldres to the sovereignty. Philip, Maximilian's son, headed the imperial troops, but was obliged to leave affairs unsettled, and a truce was arranged. Isabella, queen of Castile, had just died, and Philip hastened to Spain to claim the sovereignty in right of his wife.

In the year 1500 Louis XII. marched into Italy and took Milan, and Maximilian, unsupported by the princes of the Empire, was a helpless spectator of the French successes. In 1504 he concluded a treaty at Blois, one of the articles of which stipulated that his grandson Charles should marry Claudia, the daughter of Louis, and that she should bring Milan in dower. This treaty was soon after violated, and Claudia was married to Francis of Anjou, the heir-apparent to the French throne. An urgent appeal to the Estates of the Empire to revenge the insult was disregarded, and he was only able to raise a small army of mercenaries, at whose head he placed himself, and marched on Milan, and with the further purpose of advancing to Rome, to be crowned by the Pope. The Venetians opposed his progress, and defeated him at Catora. He returned home, and was crowned at Trient, in the name of the Pope, by Matthæus Lang, Archbishop of Salzburg, A.D. 1508. Immediately after this we find Europe, headed by the Pope, arraying itself against Venice, and Maximilian is again in the field. Venice, deserted by her Swiss mercenaries, and beaten at Aguadello by the French and at Vicenza by the imperial troops, humbled itself before the Emperor, and both he and the Pope were persuaded, incredible as it may seem, to throw France over. France, single-handed, opposed the new confederation, and her most illustrious soldier, Gaston de Foix, routed them at Ravenna (A.D. 1512), but was killed just at the moment of victory. The loss of this general was disastrous to France, and Maximilian, aided now by the Swiss, advanced upon Milan, drove out the French and placed the ducal crown on Max. Sforza's head. The following year the French again invade Lombardy, under Latremouelle. They are driven back, and the Swiss, aided by a small body of Imperialists under Ulric, Duke of Wurtemberg, follow the retreating French, and Maximilian hears, with the most exquisite satisfaction, that the imperial standards, for the first time, are planted in France, that they have advanced as far as Dijon, and that the French Government have to purchase their retirement at an immense cost.

Maximilian now entered into a league with England against France. Henry VIII. landed an army at Calais and advanced towards Terouane. Maximilian, according to Hume, entered into an engagement to bring 8,000 soldiers, and received 120,000 crowns from Henry. He was unsuccessful in obtaining them, but joined the king with a few yeomen and Flemish soldiers, and himself, to the amazement and disgust of his subjects, became a mercenary in the king's army. He wore (says Hume) "the cross of St. George, enlisted under the English king, received a hundred crowns a day as one of his subjects and captains." Hume adds that the few trained soldiers that he brought were useful in giving an example of discipline to Henry's new-levied forces, and that, though occupying the humiliating position he did, he was treated with the highest respect by the king, and really directed all the operations of the English army. They found the Earl of Shrewsbury and Lord Herbert besieging Terouane, a town on the frontiers of Picardy. The French cavalry, composed of the flower of the nobility and gentry of the kingdom, who had distinguished themselves in many brilliant actions, advanced to oppose the English army. They met at Guinegate (where, in 1479, Maximilian had defeated the French in a well-contested fight), a few miles from Terouane, and the French, seized with an unaccountable panic, turned and fled in such disorder that it acquired the name of the "Battle of the Spurs." The Duke of Longueville, commanding, Bussi d'Amboise, Clermont, Imbercourt, the Chevalier Bayard, and many other officers of distinction, were taken prisoners. Bayard, the chevalier *sans peur et sans reproche*, alone was liberated. German chroniclers aver that this was a special act of grace done by Maximilian, in recognition of Bayard's chivalric character. Bayard himself tells a different story. Finding that the day was lost, he watched his opportunity, and seeing an English officer lying down with his sword by his side, rushed to him, seized his sword; and presenting it to his throat, took him prisoner. On demanding the name of his captor, "Captain Bayard," said the knight, "who is himself your prisoner, and there is my sword." On narrating this matter to the King and the Emperor, they held, as a question of justice, that the two officers were quits, Bayard to be allowed to depart, with a six weeks' parole.*

The Emperor assembled a considerable body of troops under Count Frundsberg.

If Henry had now marched on Paris, he might have inflicted a serious injury on the French monarchy, but it suited the Emperor to waste his time on the siege of Terouane, which he caused to be razed to the ground. Its destruction did Henry no good, but relieved the Emperor from a hostile stronghold too near to his possessions in Flanders.

Three years now pass on, but no interval of peace; Count Frundsberg, in the Imperial interests, fights well in Italy, but without any very definite results. Louis XII.,

* "The Story of the Chevalier Bayard." Berville. Translated by E. Walford. Sampson Low & Co. London, 1868.

the French king, dies, and his successor, Francis I., invades Italy in person, and buys Milan from the treacherous Swiss for 300,000 crowns. Maximilian at last succeeds in raising a body of 20,000 soldiers and invades Lombardy in person (A.D. 1516). Though no longer young, his martial spirit was unabated, and he eagerly longed to celebrate his reign by some brilliant military success. He was doomed to disappointment; want of money, and the superior numbers of the enemy, compelled him to retreat and give up the hope of annexing Italian provinces to the Roman Empire. The remainder of his life was devoted to attempts to rouse his subjects to march against the Turks. It will be seen that, in spite of the acknowledged daring of Maximilian, he occasionally held aloof from enterprises which he was bound to support by material aid, letting his colleagues take the field, and only coming to the front when the danger was over and the work done.

The League of Cambray brings out in strong relief his occasional selfishness and *mala fides*. His excuse is, that where all around him (with only one or two honourable exceptions), from the Pope downwards, were uniformly perfidious, and only adhered to treaties when it was their obvious advantage to do so, he must necessarily have been sacrificed, and his empire stripped of every privilege, unless he consented to sacrifice truth to ambition.

The League of Cambray was a combination of the Pope Julius II., Louis XII. of France, the Duke of Ferrara, Ferdinand king of Aragon, Maximilian, and the Florentines, to destroy the Venetian republic (A.D. 1509). The different powers were to attack simultaneously, and from different quarters, the Venetian lands, — Maximilian to attack by way of Germany. If successful, there was to be a general partition of territory. Maximilian claimed as his share all that had ever belonged to the Empire, especially the Venetian lands. The confederates agreed that he should have Verona, Vicenza, Padua, as Emperor; as duke of Austria, they conceded to him Treviso and Friuli.

The confederate troops, as arranged, moved on the 1st of April, and in the middle of May (14th) the Venetian

E

and French armies met at Rivolta. The Venetians were
routed, and in a fortnight after the whole of the Italian
territories' were in the possession of Louis. Vicenza,
Verona, and Padua sent him their keys: Louis sent the
deputies to Maximilian, as these towns were in his territory,
as arranged. They found the Emperor at Trent, from
which place he had not moved. He now, for the first time
since he was in the purple, found himself in possession of
Italian territory, and marched at once to garrison the towns.
Treviso alone refused him admittance, and though reduced
to great extremities, remained firm to the Venetians. The
French king, having accomplished his ends, returned home,
leaving some of his troops to co-operate with Maximilian,
possibly to help him to garrison his new acquisitions. En-
couraged by the departure of Louis, the Venetians gathered
together their scattered troops and took Padua by surprise.
We have it on the authority of Guicciardini and Mezerai,
that the Pope now entered into a secret league with the
Venetians, recommended them to transfer Treviso and Padua
to the Emperor, and then to wrest them and the other
places from him as soon as a favourable opportunity
occurred. Maximilian, aided by the French troops, laid
siege to Padua, but finding it impregnable, he retired, and
returned to Germany.

The treachery of Julius II. becoming publicly known,
he and the French king were mortal enemies. The Pope
employed all the arts of cajolery to induce Henry VIII. of
England to invade France, and Louis entered into an
arrangement with Maximilian to call a general council at
Pisa (A.D. 1510), the object of which was to depose the
Pope. The Council met in the following year. It was
scantily attended, and Maximilian neither attended nor
sent his bishops, though he intended to claim the tiara if
the Council carried out the programme. The Pope pushed
on his schemes with vigour, and excommunicated the
cardinals attending it. He laid Pisa and Florence under
an interdict, the latter for allowing a hostile council to
be held in one of her cities. The Florentines forced the
priests to administer the Sacraments, but the Pisans rose

in tumult, and the Council departed quickly to Milan. The Pope called a general council to be held at the Lateran, in Rome. Delayed by the battle of Ravenna, it met, May 3, 1512.

Louis XII. was excommunicated, and France was put under an interdict. Louis' reply was given on medals he caused to be coined with the legend, "Perdam Babylonem," I will destroy Babylon. The decision of the Council of· Pisa suspending Pope Julius was published in France.

Maximilian's last act was to open the Diet at Augsburg, before which Martin Luther appeared (A.D. 1518), and had a disputation with Cajetanus, the Pope's legate.

He died at the commencement of the year 1519, and was buried at Innspruck, in the Tyrol, and his tomb is an object of veneration to this day to the Tyrolese peasants, who connect all that is glorious in their history with the exploits of Maximilian I.

It is the fashion for writers to describe Maximilian as a weak tool, incapable of governing, and degraded personally ; that even his fool Rosen ridiculed him without pity or remorse, and all owing to a spiteful remark of Macchiavelli, "that he believed that he did everything himself, and yet allowed himself to be misled from his first and best idea." A careful study of his history will show that, when not led away by an inordinate vanity,* he was a wise and observant monarch ; he knew what his country wanted, and instituted reforms of a gigantic character. He was the first to establish a regular army, and his lansquenets did good service in the field. When he could command troops he showed

---

* Dr. Dibdin relates that whilst travelling in Germany, he visited the Cathedral at Ulm, and after he had climbed to the top of its magnificent tower, with its 378 steps, his attention was drawn to the coping on the top, which showed signs at one place of being rubbed. " It was here," said the attendant, " that our famous Emperor Maximilian stood upon one leg, and turned himself quite round, to the astonishment and trepidation of his attendants ! He was a man of great bravery, and this was one of his pranks to show his courage." This story has descended to us for three centuries, and not long ago the example of the Emperor was attempted to be imitated by two Austrian officers. The first lost his balance, and was precipitated to the earth, dying the very instant he touched the ground ; the second succeeded, and de. clared himself, in consequence, " Maximilian the Second."

generalship, and it is acknowledged in the campaign with
Henry VIII., although serving as a volunteer, he really
conducted the successful campaign, ending with the battle
of Spurs. He made a tool of Henry, securing his own
wants at the expense of the English king. ·When aspiring
to the Papacy he certainly made a catspaw of Louis, as we
find, whilst the French king was expending the blood and
treasure of his country, he did nothing. Although his
courage has been doubted by none, in later years he avoided
fighting, unless obliged, kept an observant eye on what
was passing, and always tried, and not unfrequently succeeded, in profiting by the action of others. That he
allowed himself to be made a laughing-stock, even by the
court jester, is contradicted by the known fact that Rosen
was his devoted adherent, venturing his life on various
occasions in defence of his master. Luther, who certainly
owed him no goodwill, and who was bitter and sometimes
scurrilous in his denunciations of those who opposed him,
spoke respectfully of Maximilian. Thus, in his " Colloquia
Mensalia," p. 360 :—" It was a fine speech of Maximilian the
Emperor, wherewith he comforted King Philip, his son,
who deeply bewailed the death of a godly, a faithful, and
an honourable man, that was slain in a battle. His words
were these : ' Loving Philip, thou must accustom thyself
to these misfortunes; thou shalt lose yet many of those
whom thou lovest.'" At page 411 :—" When the Emperor
Maximilian made a league with the Venetians, he said :
' Three kings are in the Christian world; himself, the
French king, and the king of England. Himself [he said]
was a king of kings ; for what he imposed upon his princes,
if they were pleased therewith, then they accomplished
his will, otherwise they let it alone, thereby showing that
the princes never were in obedient subjection under the
Emperors, but did what they pleased. The French king
was a king of asses, for they did everything that he commanded them. But the king of England was a king of
people, for what he laid upon them, the same they did
willingly, and loved their king like obedient subjects.'"
Again, at page 412 :—" Of Emperor Maximilian's Mild-

ness.—As the King of Denmark sent a stately ambassador to the Emperor Maximilian, who, in the behalf of the king his master, took high honour upon himself, insomuch as the ambassador would deliver his message sitting; when the Emperor marked the same, he arose and gave him audience standing, so that the ambassador, for shame, could not remain sitting. Likewise, at another time, when an ambassador, in the beginning of his speech, was astonished and amazed at the Emperor's presence, stood mute, insomuch that he could not proceed. Then the Emperor began to discourse with him touching other affairs, giving the ambassador time to recover his spirits and deliver himself with a degree of courage."*

Luther also mentions Maximilian's good-nature, relating how a beggar stopped him and told him that, although he was only a pauper and the Emperor a rich and great man, yet they were brothers, and he was bound to administer to his necessities. The Emperor smiled, and said: "Well, if all men are brothers, here is a penny; go and ask all your other brothers for a like sum, and you will be richer than your Emperor." Maximilian was neither superstitious nor cruel. He kept as good faith in political matters as was possible in an age when public morality was unknown ; and if his private life was not unstained, his excuse must be found in the unbridled licentiousness which was exhibited in the lives of even the highest ecclesiastics.

The text (vol. i.) of "Wise King," containing the auto-biography of Maximilian, has never appeared in an English dress, and would not repay the trouble of a translation. The Editor has extracted such portions as relate to the training and domestic life of the Emperor, with the history of his marriage and the birth of his son. Maximilian treats history as a romance, and we should judge of him as living in a fool's paradise if we only knew him through his writings.

* English translation. By Captain Henry Bell. Second edition. London, 1791.

That he evinced both sense and spirit in his government we know from other sources.

Mr. Secretary Treytzsaurwein must have had great command of expression if he controlled a smile whilst writing down from the middle-aged monarch the description of his benignant face. The text of the " Wise King" is in archaic German, and the object of the Editor has been to leave it as far as possible in its quaint rendering.

P. 55, A. 1459.

How the Queen (Eleanora) gave birth to a Son.

When the time drew near of the birth of the child, there was to be seen at·times, and yet not very clearly, a comet, about which the people did talk much. The old wise king, likewise the exiled prince and all the people in the whole kingdom, called to God with great devotion that by His mercy the queen and all the people might be gladdened by her delivery. Now, if every Christian considers the great mercy God Almighty has granted to both of them at Rome in spiritual and worldly honour, with the highest royal coronation in the world, and also (considers) their devotion and meekness, how they in great divine love visited and piously honoured all the holy places in the town of Rome and else-. where, no one can doubt that God, in His mercy, has graciously heard their prayers, for all good things come from God. And on the day and at the hour of the birth of the child, the above-mentioned comet appeared much bigger than commonly, and sent forth a clear and light lustre.

Although comets generally are to be looked upon with a melancholy heart, yet this comet was pleasant to behold in its brilliancy, so that everybody's heart felt inclined to regard this appearance of the comet as a special significant omen and manifestation of the child's birth. During the afternoon of the comet the queen, by a special grant of divine mercy, gave birth to the child under little pain at the town of Newenstadt, and she was highly delighted with her delivery, for the child was a beautiful son.

This was reported with great rejoicings to the old wise king. Thereupon they began to ring all the bells for joy, and the people all over the kingdom made innumerable bonfires ; such great joy the old wise king and all the people felt about this joyful delivery.

After the child was born the comet diminished, in its splendour from that moment ; from which it was to be inferred that this comet was a sign of the future reign and wonderful achievements of the child.

And the exiled prince (Nicolaus von Vilak, Ban of Croatia, driven from his dominions by the Turks) had, when he saw that the empress was pregnant (prophesied and expressed his hope that the child to be born might revenge his wrongs upon the Turks) recognized through the comet how his speech (prophecy) was confirmed by heaven. He also desired to be godfather at the christening of the child ; to which office the old wise king appointed him, since this prince was born of a royal race. I will disclose this, that when this child came of age and into his reign, he was the most victorious and valiant ; and yet to look at his countenance he was most benignant, which certainly is strange in a valiant, nay the most valiant of men. So it is clear the comet prophesied rightly. (The sentence here is broken, and the German editor adds what does not seem much to the purpose, "remark the young king's fair benignant face.")

P. 59.

How the Old Wise King appointed several Learned Masters to instruct his Son.

Although the son of the old wise king was still young, even in his childhood, he in a short time showed such signs of excellence and such good manners, that he surpassed all the children of princes and noblemen to such an extent, that, considering his youth, everybody was astonished. And the old wise king was mightily pleased, as may easily be imagined. And he took the greatest care to impress upon him the fear of God, and notably did lay stress on these three Commandments, out of the ten which God Almighty had given to Moses:—The first, "Believe in one God;" the other, "Honour thy father and mother;" the third, "Do unto thy neighbour as to thyself." The old wise king did most earnestly desire to have him instructed in Holy Scripture, that he might thoroughly learn the three rules which ought to guide all Christian education. First, to acknowledge the laws of God, and to love Him beyond all things, for whoever hath not the fear of God will not live in eternity; the other, that he should be thankful to his father and mother, and to all those who did him good, and honour them; for ingratitude is a vice under which all other vices find shelter. The third, give to your neighbour what is due to him, because whoever doeth unrightly in his government, and conducts justice one-sidedly, will forfeit his temporal and eternal honour. And after such God-fearing deliberations of the old·wise king, he, as a true and faithful father, selected some highly learned masters, leading pious lives, to teach his son Latin, but chiefly the fear of God, and after that Holy Scripture. They taught him with great zeal. Also there were given to him as companions the children of many mighty princes and noblemen to learn with him, and to attend on him. He was first taught the obedience due from children, the duties of a king, the fear of God, and Holy Scripture, which he studied with great perseverance. He honestly endeavoured not to neglect in any way his lessons, and so not to bring upon himself punishment by his masters, as happens to other children, who are punished and beaten for their slothfulness and neglect. He would not rest until he had mastered the tasks that were set to him, and he got to know the Holy Scriptures so well, that many a time he put questions to his masters which they were not able to answer, because, although he was learned in the fundamental doctrines of Holy Scripture, his intellect which God had given him carried him beyond the teaching, as proved by the fact that he puzzled his masters. When the old wise king his father perceived this, he took him away from the study of Holy

Scripture, that he might employ his time better in learning other things. And when the masters gave up his son to the old wise king, the son, in the presence of his masters, made from his own impulse the following speech to his father : "As the stem of a tree has been planted and bent in its youth, it will remain when old ; the finer a fruit is, the more delicate will be its taste and flavour ; the more beautiful and transparent a stone, the more noble and valuable will be that precious stone." The old wise king called upon his son to explain the meaning of his speech. The son answered : "As a gardener engrafts a twig of a fruit-tree on a stem, and as the twig grows into that stem, the stem bears afterwards the fruit of the twig. Thus has been grafted into me the branch of Holy Scripture and of Christian faith, and the branch has grown into the stem, and will in the future bear fruit." And further the son said : "The finer a fruit, the better will be its flavour. Thus has been manifested to me the profit arising from gratitude and modesty implanted in my heart. That pride will be recognized at once when compared with my modesty and humility." Thirdly, the son said : "The more beautiful and transparent a stone is, the more precious is that stone : thus are rooted within myself the purity of unblemished honour, of kingly virtue, and a rooted sense of the justice of the laws of God, and from me will shine forth these virtues in my government." After this explanation, the old wise king felt great joy, and the king, as well as the masters, decided that he should henceforth be called the young wise king. Any man of learning and sense might conclude that the above speech foreshadowed the future, as during his reign in his old age he has obtained the highest kingly crown, has been a lover of the Christian Church, the dispenser of justice, the boldest and most victorious in all fights, and the most humble towards all men.

P. 62.

*How the Young Wise King from his own impulse learns
to write.*

After this young wise king had sufficiently studied Holy
Scripture, there often came into his hands some beautifully
written manuscripts. Although he need not have acquired
a particularly good handwriting, yet, after his determination
to be equal to everybody else, he undertook and practised
writing so much, and took lessons of which he never tired,
for it was only a pastime to him ; and thus he acquired by
his industry and daily exercise a particularly good handwriting, which he soon wrote very fast. Of this the old wise
king was much pleased, and the good writers were greatly
astonished that in a short time, from his own impulse and
by his industry, he should have learnt such good handwriting. And in order that people may know that his
handwriting was so good, [it should be told that] he had at
the time of his government with him a secretary, who was
·famous at the time for being the finest and most speedy
writer. One day, when this same secretary was with him,
the young wise king wrote with him for emulation, and
with respect to quickness the young wise king surpassed
the secretary. From this time is to be seen the young
wise king's steady purpose he had in all things he wished
to learn. And during the time of his reign he was never
tired of writing. He had written so much with his own
hand, that if I was to give the number of his writings on
the average, people would not believe me, for the reason of
the great wars he constantly made during his reign.

P. 63.

*How the Young Wise King learnt the Seven Liberal Arts
in a short time.*

After the young wise king had sufficiently studied Holy
Scripture, in order that he might not in his youth spend

any time in vain, the old wise king ordered his masters to
teach him the seven liberal arts, which they did with great
diligence, and showed him how no art [in a short time]
could by any man be acquired perfectly; moreover, one art
sprung from another, after the manner of a chain, which is
made of many links. From this he might learn from them,
and understand that one art, as far as learning, practice,
and work were concerned, gave a hand to another. In
order that he might learn from them, and understand gradually more of such teaching, he worked diligently at his
lessons, and learnt at the beginning grammar, as the basis
of the other six liberal arts; after that logic, then the other
five liberal arts; and in a short time he became in these
seven liberal arts unsurpassedly learned, for he understood
more of them than is set forth in books, at which his master
and [other] learned men were astonished. His masters
also thought that it would not be good nor useful to trouble
him any more with these subjects; for if you desire to teach
a man more than is needed, that is superabundance, and a
hindering of other work. And they said this to the old wise
king. He summons his son, and says to him, " I have great
pleasure about your learning, but will you act out a virtuous
and useful life?" Thereupon the son gave this answer:
" The good seed of virtue and [knowledge of] art which I
have sown by my industry will bear beautiful flowers in my
years, through which your garden shall be full of sweet
savour, and I will not let my good seed be choked with the
vile weeds, that sow themselves and grow abundantly; but
as I have sown my good seeds with eager diligence, thus
will I earnestly hoe out and destroy the vile weeds." The
old wise king understood very well the speech of his son,
and said, "Your parable is disclosed by your works, for
how great a joy has the old wise king felt in his heart and
in his mind over this son, who was brought up in obedience
to his father, and in the fear of Almighty God." And when
he came of age and into his government he fulfilled his
promise, for in all his empire people spoke of his virtues.
That was the garden with the beautiful flowers. He also
did not allow in his empire any robbery [? ED.], but through-

out his domains you could travel quite safely : the like was not to be seen in the whole world ; that is the destruction and rooting out of the bad weeds.

P. 64.

How the Young Wise King studies Secret Knowledge and Experience of the World.

After awhile, when the young wise king was with his father, the old wise king, the father said to his son these words : "Son, listen to me ; after my death you will be the possessor of many empires. Though every king is like another man, yet kings who govern themselves must know more than the princes and the people, that their government may be permanent ; and my words that I say unto you relate to experience of the world." The father did not wish during this interview to disclose everything to him, for this reason, to test the intelligence of his son. The son did not show [that he saw through his father's intention,] but he thought much, and likewise read many writings of past history, and on human nature, and of men's intentions, and of their various ranks, in which he found, with much trouble, the secret of how the world is to be governed ; all that came from his intellect, otherwise from writings alone he could not have found it out. Should I disclose herein this secret knowledge ? There is no need, for it belongs only to kings. After that the wise young king came to his father, and said, " Father, I have thought of your fatherly advice with respect to experience of the world, and have discovered within me that I ought to know such things, and have practised much and diligently by reading and reflecting in my mind, that I hope I have mastered the secret knowledge and experience of the world." And he began to speak to his father about the world and its government, beginning with the (Diets) States, from the Pope to the Cardinal, from the Cardinal to the Bishop, from the Bishop to the Priests, from the Priests to the Monks, from the Monks to the Nuns ; after that from the Kings to the Archdukes, from the Archdukes to the

Princes, from the Princes to the Counts, from the Counts
to the Lords, from the Lords to the Knights, from the
Knights to the Nobility, from the Nobility to the Burghers,
from the Burghers to the Peasants ; and spoke to his father
of five articles :—the first, of the omnipotence of God ; the
second, of the influence of planets ; the third, of the mode
of reasoning of men ; the fourth, of too great mildness in
governing ; the fifth, of too much severity in power ; and
after these words the son went on to say, " And therefore
I will in future keep and preserve in my heart these words,
Be moderate ! and I have no doubt what I have considered
[determined on] that will happen to me a hundredfold,—
I don't mean a hundredfold, but it will happen to me in
countless number [of times]." And when the old wise king
had heard the words of his son, he thanked merciful God,
and said, " Almighty God, Thou who alone art merciful,
keep my seed [son] in Thy pleasure, then my joy will be
increased."

When the wise young king came of age and into his
powerful government, he never refused any man anything
without making sufficient inquiry; he even has not been
satisfied with the inquiry, but has looked at the works
[inquired into the applicant's character,] and never allowed
passion to influence his conduct, but has viewed [human]
nature with [its mixture] of good and evil; thus confirming
his words, *Be moderate !* This is so great a virtue, so great
[rare] in men, that in his praise a special book ought to be
written.

P. 65.

How the Young Wise King learns the Art of Astrology.

After the young wise king had reflected on the secret
knowledge of experience, and discovered it in good measure, as has been told before, he revolved in his mind how
he should strongly desire to acquire a knowledge of the
stars and of their influence, [as seen] by their effects ; otherwise he might not be able to learn the nature of mankind
perfectly, which might be a disadvantage to him in the

secret knowledge of the experience of the world. He
thought about what is hidden from others with especial
attention, and after that invited to him the most learned
doctor of astrology [Georgius Tanstetter, Professor of Astro-
nomy,] and learnt very diligently from him this art, and
listened eagerly to the influences of the skies and the effect
of the stars, from which men receive their nature and being
[character], also the order and circles of heaven. Of this
art much might be written. In a short time he acquired
a sufficient foundation of this art, for from him nothing was
hidden by the doctor, and he got so far that he would not
be satisfied with astrology as relating to the known stars,
and he put before the master this article [problem], viz.,
after the astrology of the known stars, and after having
seen the strange, astonishing effects upon the earth, there
ought to be some more stars that in this art were yet
undiscovered and unknown, that had also effects upon
[human] natures. On this problem much has been written,
and all astrologers have to instruct themselves about it.
Thereupon the doctor asked the young wise king whether
he admitted the influence of stars. This he did for the
purpose, to find if he had acquired the basis of the art.
The young wise king gave the doctor this answer: "My
father is a king, and governs his people through his captains, chancellors, councillors, and servants; but the power
he has in his hand." As soon as the doctor heard these
words from him, he said, "I do not find fault with your
learning, for with your answer you surpass my question,
and you want my teaching no more. And the young wise
king has confirmed this his art during his life in his government; for whenever an important matter happened to him,
he acted in it after giving proper time to it, [the result]
sometimes arrives slowly. This is not the usual course of
men, for many drop into misfortunes through rashness, and
this the young wise king avoided. I call the young wise
king in his actions not a man, but I call him the Time. He
always acted for a certain [defined] reason, which surpasses
[ordinary] men's [method], and he has acted according to
time and circumstances, &c. (So ends this chapter, which is

certainly very obscure; but it must be remembered that
Maximilian was not a metaphysician.—ED.)

P. 71.

How the Young Wise King learnt the duties of a Public Secretary.

At one time the old wise king, contemplating the course
of the world, found out, from his own experience in governing, where a mighty king, who was not conversant with and
equal to the duties of a Chancellor and Secretary's office,
might at some time or other be at a disadvantage, for this
reason, that a king should not disclose his intentions, or
place his confidence in another. It is well known how the
old wise king, for such reason, summoned his son to him,
and employed him to do such writing as belongs to the
duties of chancellor and secretary, which is the chief part
of every king's government, in order that he might acquire
the principles of government, and might learn to distinguish
selfish people. The old wise king employed him very much
in all these things, and the son was very assiduous, and
in a short time he learnt the principal duties. His father
saw this with particularly great satisfaction, and once said
to him, "Son, do you understand the principles of government by writing?" The son answered: "If a king puts
his trust in one man, and believes in his actions and fine
sayings, then this man reigns, and not the king. If a king
does not find out the unfaithful and selfish, he will have
his treasure and empire in confusion. If a king does not
love the truthful and those that live honourably, such a
king is an oppressor of his people, and a rooter out of
justice." The father listened gladly to this speech, [finding]
that the son understood the principles of government; and
when the young wise king came into years and power, he
employed a good many secretaries, to all of whom he gave
plenty of work, and always educated these secretaries from
their youth, according to his own [method] will. He also
never allowed a letter to be sent, whether the matter was

small or important, unless he had first read it, and he signed all letters with his own hand. This king has ruled so assiduously, that the description of such another reign is not to be found. He was also so unsurpassed in drawing up letters, and in his powers of memory, that he often dictated to nine, ten, eleven, and twelve secretaries at the same time, to each a separate letter ; and all the government of all his kingdoms and lands was done by him alone, besides all the great wars he made against foreign nations and countries.

P. 75.

How the Young Wise King learned Painting.

Once upon a time the young wise king heard an old wise man say, that he who intended to be a good general and commander of armies ought to be able to paint, and to have a particular knowledge of the art. These words the young wise king kept in his mind, and began forthwith to learn to paint. He studied very diligently, but it was only when he had got so far as to paint landscapes of the country that he partly understood the words of the wise old man, viz., that every great ruler and general ought to be able to paint. But for what reason it is not fit for me to disclose in this book, nor to write about it, but it ought to be kept to kings and commanders alone. Now when the wise young king understood the utility and meaning of the art of painting, which were hidden to him in the speech of the wise old man, he exhibited so much perseverance in the study of painting, that he learned sufficiently well how to paint, and now comprehended the real principles of painting. This young king was, however, diligent in all things he undertook, and in his years and government painting was of great use to him, since he employed many painters, led powerful armies, sustained great struggles, and was the most valiant and most invincible ; for all these achievements he made use of the art of painting, and it brought him [great] advantages. He also used paintings in many other things,—in tournaments, constructions, and inventing new works; by means of it he accomplished that which otherwise he would have been unable to achieve. Every one who knows anything about these matters will understand what is not described here. He also supported great artists in painting and carving, and has caused many ingenious works to be painted and carved, which will remain in this world in memory of him, though some are under feigned names.

P. 78.

How the Young Wise King learned Music and to Play on Stringed Instruments.

At one time the king thought of King David, how the Almighty God had shown him so much mercy, and he read the Psalms, in which he found very often the words, "Praise God with songs and with harps;" so he thought how mightily pleasing those praises were to God. Then he took unto him the history of King Alexander, who had conquered so many peoples and countries, and read his history, in which is written that King Alexander was very often moved by the songs of minstrels and by the happy sounds of the harps, [so that his spirit was raised] and he vanquished his enemies. By that the heart of the young king was moved a great deal, and he determined earnestly to follow King David and King Alexander in offering praises to God; and he learned with the greatest zeal and perseverance all manner of song and music of string-instruments, regarding as the two gravest duties the praise of God and the vanquishing of his enemies, which are the two highest virtues of a king. You may imagine, since this king undertook such a thing, and set his mind on it, how much care he took with it, and how he liked it.

So now, with his anxiety and facility for learning, he understood in a short time the fundamental principles of singing and of playing on all stringed instruments, and when he came into his most august government he followed first the practice of King David in the praise of God. He

G

established such a choir, with such agreeable and happy songs, delightful to hear, of the human voice, and with such agreeable harps, played after a new fashion, and with sweet stringed instruments, that he left far behind him the efforts of all other kings in this kind of thing, and so that nobody could be compared to him, which choir he sustained and kept, as is the custom of such a great kingly court as his, and used the same choir only for the praise of God in the Christian churches.

After that he began, following the example of Alexander, with the happy string music to excite to boldness, and surpassed both Alexander and Cæsar in his victories. I will show this quite plainly: Though Alexander the Great has conquered many lands and has delighted in the playing of stringed instruments, nevertheless the young wise king has established such delightful, skilful fifers, and invented all sorts of drums, and used such in his wars when he has gone against his enemies, and with these fifes and drums he has not only regaled the human heart, but the sound from them has filled the air; and with these has the young wise king not only conquered many countries, but with their aid he has fought his principal battles, and fought his enemies and beaten them. And also Julius Cæsar, who has only become emperor through his war feats. Nevertheless, he had only one party opposed to him; but this young wise king has had to fight many enemies, of whom I will give you the names of a few; as the king of France, the powerful peoples of Switzerland, the potent dominion of Venice, the emperor of the Turks, the kingdom of Hungary, the kingdom of Bohemia, and other enemies, whom I may not mention here. Surrounded by such enemies, he has so managed that he has invaded their lands, and not they his Austria. If any should criticise these writings, I know that those learned in history, and particularly in the reign of the wise young king, will say he speaketh truly; if any without experience and learning should contradict these sayings, he will cover himself with ridicule.

P. 102, A. 1473.

How a mighty King, called the King of the Flaming Iron,* had an only daughter, and could not agree with the Old Wise King.

Now there was not far from the kingdom of the old wise king a noble king, called the King of the Flaming Iron, holding much land, and mighty in men. He was also called Charles, Duke of Burgundy. The duke was a mighty warrior, and so powerful, that at one time he made war on the powerful king of France, according to his pleasure, and wrested from this king the grant of the fief of the great

---

* A nickname, originating in the chain of the order of the Golden Fleece. This order was instituted on the 10th of January, 1429, by Philip the Good, Duke of Burgundy, and Earl of Flanders. He took for his device, Autre n'auray,—I will have (or wear) none other. It was founded at Bruges, in Flanders, on the day of Philip's marriage with his third wife, the Infanta Isabella of Portugal. It ranks next to the Garter.

"On days of ceremony the knights wear the collar, which is composed of double steels, interwoven with flint stones, emitting sparks of fire (the whole enamelled in their proper colours), at the end whereof hangs on the breast a golden fleece. The fusils are joined two and two together, as if they were the double BB's (the cipher of Burgundy). There are four great officers under the Grand Master; viz., the Chancellor, the Treasurer, the Register, and a' King-of-Arms, called Toison d'or."—CLARK'S *History.*

The badge consists of a golden fleece suspended from a flint stone, which is surrounded with flames of gold. This the knights wear round the neck, suspended from a ponceau, or fire-coloured ribbon, of the breadth of two fingers, and it hangs upon the breast. When the order was first instituted, the knights (who were at first limited to twenty-five) were obliged to wear the collar daily, but Charles V. substituted the ribbon above mentioned in lieu thereof. The habit consists of a long mantle and a cap of crimson velvet, which are lined with white silk. The mantle is entirely bordered with the insignia of the order, viz., flint-stones and fire-steels, disposed alternately. The former are surrounded with flames of fire, and the whole is worked in a rich embroidery of gold. When the order was first instituted, the Grand-mastership was inalienably attached to the earldom of Flanders. Afterwards the King of Spain and the Emperor equally claimed the Grand-mastership, both claiming to represent the earls of Flanders; the King of Spain as *Heir-General,* and the representative of the Infanta Maria Theresa, daughter of Philip IV.; the Emperor contests it as heir in tail male, representing the oldest branch of the House of Austria, which was engrafted upon those of Flanders and Burgundy by the marriage of Maximilian with Mary of Burgundy. The decorations, or insignia, and the statutes are the same in Spain and Germany.—ED.

country of Flanders, and held it independently. He also had jurisdiction over the strong country of Guelderland. He overpowered and conquered it by the sword, and also drove the Duke of Lorraine from his possessions. This same king of the Flaming Iron had no children except an only daughter, and had heard much of the young wise king, of his wisdom, repute, glory, and popularity, so that he took a great liking to him. For he was a popular hero himself, and therefore felt a secret great pleasure in the wise young king's wisdom and renown; but at the same time the king of the Flaming Iron felt a secret jealousy of the wise old king, the father of the young wise king, for the reason that he thought himself equal to the old wise king, and he dared to form a party of his own in his kingdom, thinking that he would thus gain in war a glory beyond that of any other king in this world.

P. 103, A. 1473.

How the Old Wise King and the King of the Flaming Iron met to marry their children.

After the king of the Flaming Iron had dared to form a conspiracy in the kingdom of the old wise king, as before mentioned, and when the old wise king came to hear of this, he called a council, meaning to frustrate the intentions of the king of the Flaming Iron. Several princes and persons of consequence stepped in, and arranged that the two kings should meet in a large town called Trèves, belonging to the old wise king, and there it was agreed that the old wise king should help the king of the Flaming Iron to obtain elsewhere glory and success [an equivalent], for the said king of the Flaming Iron was rich in money and land, and was a great warrior, and therefore the two kings should marry their children. For the old wise king had an only son, and the king of the Flaming Iron had an only daughter, called Maria. But there were people who did not like to see this marriage concluded, and when they heard of it they practised intrigues, and set mischief between the two kings, bringing it about with great subtlety, so that the two kings separated in hostility, and their negotiations at that time came to nothing.

P. 105.

But the two kings sat in council together for a long time, until at last they both went away in mutual agreement. But at the first onslaught, and during the time the two kings were sitting in council, many a proud knight was killed on both sides, and many others besides, the greater part, however, upon the water, and others during the attack and the tumult. For there was on both sides lying against each other a great army, which is not everywhere to be kept in order, as soldiers certainly will know.*

A. 1475-77.

How the King of France, also some Princes and Lords, made an Alliance against the King of the Flaming Iron, and went into his Empire, and the King of the Flaming Iron remained dead in a battle.

Whilst the king of the Flaming Iron made war against the old wise king, the king of France, who at that time was very powerful in men and ready money, undertook and made an alliance with some princes, and lords, and communities that belonged to the old wise king, against the king of the Flaming Iron. These caused the king of the Flaming Iron great annoyance in his kingdom ; and after he had come to terms with the old wise king, as I have described above, and went back again, he undertook to revenge himself on the king of France. He obtained against him a great victory ; he also attacked some territory and mountains of the Germans.

Now there was a powerful king in the Tyrol ; he was called Archduke Sigmund of Austria ; he was the next of

* Battle of Neuss.

kin by the male line of the old wise king. This king in
the Tyrol possessed in the province where the king of the
Flaming Iron made war some fine lands, called Alsace,
Sungen, Breisgeu, and Phiert, and therein a valiant host,
horse and foot, and would not allow the war that the king
of the Flaming Iron made against some Germans, and *lent
great assistance* to the people called the Swiss (who were
his inheritance) by means of an army of horse and foot,
and with all the rest of his allies. This army went with
the Swiss against the king of the Flaming Iron, and had
three great contests with this king, and gained everywhere
the victory: the first fight was at Granson, the other fight
at Morta, the third fight at Nancy; and in the third and
last fight the king of the Flaming Iron was killed. Every
one may himself imagine how many people were killed in
the three great battles. This king of the Flaming Iron left
behind his wife and an only legitimate daughter, and no
child besides, about which I will write later on.

*How the Death of the King of the Flaming Iron was an-
nounced to the Old and Young Queen, and how they
mourned.*

After a short time sad news came to the old queen how
her lord and husband, the king of the Flaming Iron,
was killed in battle; this was also announced to his only
daughter. By this news the two queens were grieved with
great pains, and made a heartrending wailing, and not
without ground, as every one may himself imagine. Though
the two queens were surrounded by great grief and mourning, yet the great disturbance required them to consider
and to prevent further invasion that might happen to them
in their kingdom and lands, after this accident and defeat.
How greatly were these two queens oppressed with grief
and sorrow! Thereupon they summoned and wrote to all
their States, who came without delay, and brought their
men and followers, horse and foot, in order to defend their
kingdom and countries. The two queens also sent an
excellent embassy to the above-mentioned alliance, in

which the king of the Tyrol was the most powerful, and
got reconciled with almost all of them. The king of Tyrol
acted well and kingly towards the two queens, for he informed his relatives that it was not kingly nor honest to
insult the two queens, a lonely widow and a virgin, with
further war, and he induced his relatives who were in the
alliance not to make any more war against the two
queens ; but the king of France, who was not in this
alliance, made against the two queens an unwarrantable
and unkingly war, of which I will write later on.

*How the Old and Young Queen of the Flaming Iron, after
the advice of their States, sent to the Old Wise King's
Son to take the Young Queen in matrimony.*

The noble, beautiful young queen of the Flaming Iron
was an heiress of all kingdoms and lands that her father had
left behind. Now there was much courting for this powerful
and noble beautiful queen ; viz., there were twelve persons,
the greatest and most noble in the world, and every one of
them was the equal of the young queen in nobility. But
the above-mentioned two queens heard many reports of the
praise, glory, and worthiness of the old wise king. They
also remembered how their lord, the king of the Flaming
Iron, in his lifetime had borne a special love and inclination
towards the young wise king, and had often said of him,
the young wise king was the noblest and worthiest, and no
one equalled him. This they had kept in their hearts ; and
the young queen conceived first a special inclination and
love for the young wise king, for this queen had in her a
kingly mind, that she would not take a husband unless he
were great in nobility, and no one his equal in worthiness,
and remembered her father's worth ; for she well knew if her
father did praise a man that there was something in him.
Therefore she thought she could not doubt that the young
wise king was the noblest and worthiest ; and these two
queens, mother and daughter, therefore resolved that the
daughter should not take any other husband but the young
wise king ; but they intended to do this under the advice

of their States, and summoned their States to them, and represented to them the twelve persons who coveted the hand of the young queen. They also discovered to the States, though these knew it themselves, the great wars they were obliged to make against their enemies, and that therefore she, the young queen, stood in need of a worthy man ; and because her lord and father, the king of the Flaming Iron, in his lifetime had given glory and praise to the young wise king, that he was the noblest and worthiest, her mother and herself had agreed together that she should take the young wise king before all others for her husband; but they wanted to do this only by their [the States'] advice. The States considered and deliberated amongst each other. Now every one was upon the side of that one whom the queen wished for. Some acted thus for a gift, some for other reasons, but most of them were bought over with money. From this it may be concluded that some would take the money whether the queen married well or badly. But the common States [the whole States] considered the matter carefully, and resolved that the young queen should take the young wise king for her husband, and went to the two queens, and represented to them that they thought this marriage useful and honourable for the young queen, also for her kingdom and lands, for these three reasons :—the first, the young wise king was the noblest, and the only heir of his father the old wise king ; and besides, his father was, as to royal honour, the highest and most powerful king in this world. The other reason, the young wise king had the glory and praise to be the worthiest youth. The third reason, because the mind and will of the young queen was inclined to this noblest blood, this marriage should be concluded, and no other marriage should be entered upon. Thereupon they agreed with one voice that the two queens should write to the young wise king how he had been selected before all other kings as a husband for the young queen. Thereupon a letter was sent to the youth, and the messenger did not tarry, but rode quickly on until he came to the young wise king, and brought him the message. Now the king of France also

had a son : this king tried in many ways to obtain from
the young queen that she should take his son, and spent
secretly much money with the intention of obtaining the
young queen for his son by cunning ; and when the king of
France learned that the young queen bore love and affection
towards the young wise king, he undertook to calumniate
the youth to the young queen, and sent secretly a message
to the young queen to tell her secretly how the young wise
king was an ill-formed man, and she ought not to harm
herself by marrying him. His son [he said] was a handsome, well-made youth, and her equal ; him she should
choose and take for her husband. Now his son was short
and hunchbacked, and had a large head and short legs,
and was called from his malformation the hunchbacked
king. But the young queen would not hear this message
secretly, but answered she would like to hear it publicly,
for she heard nobody secretly by herself, but always acted
under advice of her mother and the States. After this
answer the embassy went back again to their king without
being heard.

*How the Young Wise King tells his Father of the message
from the Young Queen of the Flaming Iron.*

The messenger whom the two queens of the Flaming
Iron had sent to the young wise king came to the youth
and delivered him the letter which the two queens had
written to him, and said to him these words : "You are
chosen and selected to take in matrimony the noble, beautiful, and young queen of the Flaming Iron." The youth
heard these words carefully, and received the letter from
the messenger and read this letter at once, in which there
was written the whole thing which the messenger had told
him in few words. Thereupon he ordered his people to
take the messenger into cheerful quarters, and to do him
great honour. The young wise king went to his father,
the old wise king, and informed him of the message and
of the letter the two queens of the Flaming Iron had sent
him, and asked his advice as father, for it is just and decent

H

that a son should act after the advice of his father. This message the father listened carefully to, and considered the matter in every way; and after he had taken the matter in careful consideration, he told his son the following three articles in a few words:—firstly, the honour of the marriage; secondly, the usefulness of the possessions; thirdly, the care he should take to obtain all this, and left to his son the choice, and left it to him either to go or stay at home. Thereupon the young wise king considered shortly, and spoke to his father: "My father, nothing is better than real honour, and nothing more pleasing to God Almighty than to live in His commandments; how then could I obtain real honour in the world but by this noble queen of honours? how could I serve God better than by putting forth my hand after His divine commandment in eternal remembrance?" When the father heard from his son these words of great wisdom his heart jumped within him with admiration of his son's wisdom, and he said to his son, "If you will go in the manner you have represented to me, I will give you my permission. But since I have now on my hands a war against the *Green King*, I will give you for some time my army, that you may learn to make war, for this reason, that if you come to the government of the queen's country, you may know how to deal with your enemies." This the son accepted very gladly. Thereupon the young wise king summoned the messenger of the two queens, and gave him a letter, in which he wrote friendly to the two queens with many thanks, and a special wish that they might be constant in the choice of her future. He also informed them that he intended to prepare and to come to them in a short time with devotion, and in royal honours. This he did, as will be described later on.

How the Young Wise King, with permission of his Father,
went against the Green King.

There was a king called the Green king, whose kingdom
touched the old wise king's kingdom, and this Green king
undertook to make war against some lands of the old wise
king.   And when the old wise king would not let his son
go to the queen of the Flaming Iron unless he learned before
the art of war, the young wise king had a great desire to try
his young, noble, and worthy hand in the field against his
enemy, and to perform in his youth real and terrible feats
of war, and asked thereupon his father to allow him to
make an onslaught on the people of the Taertschen, who
followed the Green king.   This his father did not like to
allow him, for this reason, that he was his only son ; still
his father gave him the permission, but under the advice
of his chiefs and councillors of war, and he gave to his
son letters to the captains of his army and camp.   These
letters the young wise king accepted from his father, and
went without delay to these captains and gave them the
letters, whereupon they obeyed him.   The young wise
king did not tarry, but he went at once with the artillery
before a fortress wherein a people of the Taertschen was
lying who followed the Green king, and ordered to work
upon this fortress severely with the artillery.

How the Green King sent an Army into the Old Wise King's
land, which the Young Wise King put to flight.

When the Green king learned that the young wise king
with the artillery had gone before a fortress, the Green
king assembled an army.   Now this king had a captain,
whom he sent with this army into the old wise king's
country, where they caused much damage.   As soon as
the young wise king got news about this, he took with him
an armed train and a part of the foot, and marched day
and night against this enemy to overtake and to beat them.
Now there was one among the army of the young wise

king who warned the above-named Green captain. This
Green captain began to fly with his army in such a
manner, that many of the Green army being tired had to
stay behind: some were killed by frost, some had their
hands and feet frozen. But the young wise king, notwithstanding, hastened after him into the Green king's kingdom,
and did in this kingdom much burning and pillaging, and
thereupon he went back again to the camp.

P. 112.

*How the Old Wise King summoned his Son, the Young
Wise King, and sent him to the Young Queen in order
to marry her.*

Thereupon, after the young wise king had done the
burning and pillaging in the Green kingdom, the old wise
king summoned his son to him. Though the young wise
king would have liked to make war a little longer against
the Green king, yet the old wise king accepted a truce from
the Green king, and sent thereupon his son the young wise
king away to the noble, beautiful queen of the Flaming
Iron, and got him up in royal honours, with many knights
and great nobles who went with him. Now the young wise
king had a far way to go to the young queen, and prepared himself, likewise his knights and nobles, in the costliest manner for all emergencies. The young wise king
and all the host that went with him took leave of the old
wise king as it was fit to do. It is easily to be imagined,
where a son goes from his father on a precarious journey,
that fatherly and filial love will not be hidden away;
thus it also happened at this parting. But these kings
put forth their hands again and again at [in recognition of] the highest royal honours, which indeed they obtained everywhere. There came also on the road to the
young wise king many archbishops, bishops, and princes,
with a great number of knights, who went with the young
king unto the above-mentioned young queen.

(53)

P. 113, A. 1477.

*How the Young Wise King came to the Young Queen, and
how he was received.*

When the wise young king was on his way * to go to
the above-mentioned young queen, this fact was told to
the two queens above mentioned. Thereupon they felt
great joy, and forthwith called together their States, and
let them also know the intentions of the young wise
king. The Estates did not tarry, but came without delay
to the two queens, when they held a council how the young
wise king should be received. Thereupon they wrote to
the young wise king that he should come to the town
called Ghent, whither the two queens with their States
would also come. Then, as soon as the letter was sent to
the young wise king, the two queens, together with their
States, went to the town above mentioned, and waited
there for the arrival of the young king, who after a few
days came thither, and on the day when he entered the
town, there rode to meet him, firstly, the burghers of the
said town splendidly dressed ; after them the whole assembly
of princes, bishops, prelates, counts, lords, knights, and followers a great number ; then there went to meet him the
whole clergy, with holy emblems in procession, and all
the people of the town, and received the young king with
great dignity, high honour, and especial rejoicings, and he
rode into the town amidst a great crowd, in magnificent
attire, with royal honours ; and all who saw him were particularly delighted with his handsome, young, upright figure,
and the people said they had never beheld a more beautiful
young lord, and they wondered very much indeed at the
old wise king his father sending his son in his early youth
so far into a foreign country, and the young king was led to
his dwelling, which was gorgeously prepared for him. The

* Commines says that Maximilian had to halt at Cologne, being short of
funds, and had to wait there until the Princess Mary sent him enough to pass
on to Ghent.—ED.

two queens then ordered a magnificent banquet to be prepared towards evening, and sent for the young king and
many distinguished persons to come to it, where the two
queens wanted to receive him in person ; and before he went
to the said banquet, he dressed himself and embellished
himself with costly clothes and jewellery, and went with
his princes, nobles, and knights in royal attire. Now it
was nightfall, and there was a great crowd, for which reason
they were obliged to have many torches, for everybody
wanted to see the young wise king.   In the mean time the
two queens were alone by themselves in a chamber, and
said to each other that they also should like to see the
young king secretly. Thereupon the old queen,* the young
queen's mother, disguised herself in common clothes, and
went secretly, dressed in white, out of the chamber into
the hall, whither the young wise king was to come. Now
the crowd of the people was so great, that the old queen
was not able for a long time to get through the throng,
and had to obtain trustworthy and secret assistance. When
she had passed through the people, the young wise king had
just entered the hall, and when he was shown to her, she
would not at first believe that he was the young wise king,
for she thought he was too handsome, and fancied she had
never seen so comely a youth, and waited and wanted to
see which was the wise young king. Now she saw upon
the same handsome youth all honour was bestowed, and he
was being surrounded by the most powerful archbishops
and princes, and that the same youth was the real young

* The story of the two queens, viz., the dowager of Burgundy, being in a
chamber consulting with each other how to receive Maximilian, must have
been a pure romance.   Commines and other writers mention the removal of
the stepmother of Mary when the French king betrayed her letters. As Commines was cousin to Madame de Hallewin, first lady of the bedchamber to the
princess, he had every opportunity of knowing. He does state that the widow
of Charles the Bold was in communication with the commissioners sent by
Frederick to call upon Mary to fulfil the marriage with Maximilian, as she had
sent a letter to that effect, and enclosed a diamond ring. Mary avowed the
letter and the ring, and without consulting any one, declared her intention of
marrying Maximilian, as she had acted in obedience to her father's commands.
—ED.

wise king. After that the old queen went hastily to her daughter, the young queen, into the chamber, and spoke to her with the utmost impressiveness : " O daughter ! I never saw a more handsome youth than the young wise king is, and this young king is to be your lord and husband, and no other one." From this it may be gathered that the king of France and his son, for whom he had secretly sought the hand of the young queen, were exposed to ridicule, as I have observed before. For the young wise king was a tall youth, perfectly formed in body and build [literally bones] ; he had a handsome, winning face, and peculiarly beautiful fair hair. He was called, on account of his beauty and wisdom, the young wise king with the benignant face.

As now the young wise king was standing in the middle of the hall, the two queens went up to him and received him with royal honours, with great rejoicings and friend-ship. Also, as soon as the young queen looked at the young wise king she felt great delight at his personal appearance, and her heart was satisfied with him, and inflamed towards him with honourable love. And at the same hour they, with her permission [Q. the old queen's?], conversed together confidentially about the marriage, and settled the matter with mutual joy ; and after that the banquet was brought to an end with great rejoicings. How full of enjoyment was this banquet, during which such a royal marriage between the two noblest, mightiest, and handsomest persons was resolved upon !

P. 115, A. 1477.

How the Young Wise King and the Young Queen of the Flaming Iron were united in Marriage.

The day after the marriage of the young wise king with the queen of the Flaming Iron was resolved upon, the cathe-dral of the town was most beautifully decorated, into which the young king and queen were conducted with great royal honours ; and there went with them all archbishops, bishops, princes, counts, lords, knights, and followers, and the whole

Diet, richly dressed and decked with jewellery in their vestments. Then one archbishop preceded all the others, and led the young king and queen up to the altar, and pronounced over them some pious prayers; and when he was about to unite them in marriage, the archbishop began to speak these words: "O Lord our God, knower of hearts, blessed are the men that live in Thy commandments," and some more pious words, and thereupon joined them in holy matrimony with great solemnity and devotion, according to the law and ordination of the holy Christian Church; and after the joining in matrimony was over, the archbishop prayed to God that He might grant to these two persons four things:—to prolong their lives, to give health to their bodies, issue to their union, and victory over their enemies, and spoke over them many devout prayers besides. After that, the archbishop commenced holy mass, which was concluded with great solemnity; and after mass was said, the king and queen were led before the high altar, where they knelt down with great devotion, and the archbishop said again many pious prayers over them, and called to God with these words: "Lord, behold Thy creatures, and the mercy Thou hast bestowed on these two people in this world in royal honours; keep them in meekness for the salvation of their souls, and grant them victory over all their enemies, faithfulness in their royal union, and that they may live in Thy divine light in justice and honour, and rejoice in these in Thee for ever and ever. Amen!"

Thereupon they began to sing the Te Deum Laudamus with loud musical accompaniments, and left the church in royal order, for the wedding feast that was prepared with respect to eating and drinking in the costliest manner. And during the banquet there was much music and fine singing, wonderful joy, and many pretty banquets; and all that day was passed solely with the costly wedding banquet and its rejoicings.

P. 116, A. 1477.

How the wedding festivities above mentioned were kept up for many days with great rejoicings, and how people made merry with racing, tilting, tournaments, and other knightly games, after the fashion of different nations, and whatever might be imagined of knightly games, [sustained] most magnificently and honourably, and with the greatest cost, of which it would be possible to relate a great deal; but I will leave off, or it would prevent me from talking of other things I have mentioned herein, and will now number the mightiest countries the queen possessed, and the young wise king took under his sway; viz., the two countries, Upper and Lower Burgundy, Luxemburg, and Tischuy; the three countries, Brabant, Lorraine, and Guelderland; the five countries, Hainault, Holland, Zeeland, Flanders, and Artois; the six countries, Picardy, Friesland, Zutphen, Namur, Salines, and Malines; besides many other countries, dominions, towns, and castles, more than I can here number or name. I have only described by name the most powerful and populous countries, in order that people may recognize the great power of this young queen; and all these other countries the young wise king took also, and governed them well and royally, and kept and protected them by his valiant hand.

P. 164, A. 1485.

How a Town [Ghent—ED.] of the Brown Company* [Nether-lands—ED.] began a Conspiracy against the Young Wise King, and how the Wise King punishes them for it with the sword.

After the young wise king had conquered the land of the Brown company, he kept some thousands of his best

* The Editor of this reproduction has followed the English custom of speaking of the Wise King, but learned authorities in Germany invariably call Maximilian the White King. Hence, probably, Maximilian's mode of

I

men around him, because he dared not yet trust the Brown company (on account of some brutalities German soldiers had committed in Ghent), and the young wise king, seeing his danger, simulated flight, and the people of the town followed him, but were repulsed, and barricaded themselves with chains and vehicles. [The following takes place in the town of Ghent, between the castle and St. Pharahilde's church.] Now it was very dark, and the king thought the matter over [as to his position]; there were on one side many people, and strong chains and barricades, and cannon behind; on the other hand he had to fight, [forced] by hunger and thirst, for no man could get any food for him and his people, except dirty water. [The bishop of the town tried all he could to reconcile the parties, but in vain.] And thus remained friend and enemy the whole night opposite to each other in angry mind. The young wise king kept the enemy in constant fear by feigned attacks, in consequence of which they became very tired, for they were heavily armed, also they were never without the fear of a flight of their troops. At the same time the young wise king and his followers could obtain no food before the enemy. Then the young wise king held a council with his particular friends about what they should do in the morning, and they resolved to attack the great number [the troops in the town]. And when morning came, he advanced with his White [Austrians—ED.] company towards them up to a projection [corner of a street], lest they might do some harm with their artillery. Thereupon the great crowd of the Browns sent to the young wise king and asked for mercy, that he might pardon them, that they would withdraw, and that he [also] should withdraw. That he refused to do, for he wanted them to surrender without

describing kings and peoples by colours. In Dr. Heindrich Merz's explanatory notes to Weisser's "Bilder Atlas zur Weltgeschichte," the following passage occurs in reference to Weiss-Kunig: "The contents consist of vapid flattery (geschmaclose lobhudelei) of the *White King*, who far surpasses all his adversaries, whom he represents under different colours." The king of France, Louis XI., he called the Blue King; Matthias of Hungary, the Green King; the Netherlanders, the Brown people; the Austrians, the White people.

terms ; this they would not do either; therefore the king advanced in order to fight, and after he had made three steps, and was marching against the enemy, some one from the ranks exclaimed to him to stand still, for some of his people were dispersed, and order was broken. Thereupon the young wise king stepped back to see how this had happened. A priest had arrived with an altar-stone, and put this altar-stone on some large trestle near the ranks, and read holy mass before it ; then the greater part of his people knelt down ; the young wise king also knelt down and heard mass with his people. After that he re-arranged order, and found his people willing to fight. In the mean time the furious populace of the Browns had reflected, and gave themselves up to the king's mercy in body and goods, and went to their quarters. The king's men also went to their quarters. Thereupon the young wise king took some of the Browns who had set up the rebellion and carried on the intrigues, to the number of twenty-eight, and ordered them to be executed by the sword, and about a hundred to be expelled from the town and the country : these fled to the Blue king [Louis XI. of France—ED.]. All the others he pardoned, and took no money from them, in order to regain favour with the people.

P. 225, A. 1488.

How the Blue King arranges a Treachery, by which the Wise King is taken prisoner.

Because the young wise king everywhere was victorious against his enemies, the Blue king was angry, and won over to his side, by buying with his great treasures, a powerful captain [Hanns Kopenall], the best whom the wise young king had with him, and promised him, besides much more money, also fortresses, castles, and land ; the same captain was also for ever to have and to reign over the wise young king's lands and people. This captain deserted from the wise young king, and gathered round him a great number of bad people, and amongst them were many of the brawlers [modern *rowdies*], and he gave to these people much money, and promised them to make them the lords for ever, and were also called the Black and revolted White lot, and each of these plotted against his comrade how he might betray and sell him; and they held a council, and thought they should not be able to carry their object, unless they deprived the wise young king of his life, since he was too wise for them, and might frustrate their plans. Thus they began to intrigue together, the pious and the wicked, and once, by fair words and lies, with great cunning and treachery, they got him into a town, [thus] carrying out their design, and surprised the young wise king unexpectedly in his house, and put him and the most excellent of his captains and counsellors into prison, with the intention of killing the young wise king, also his captains and counsellors; but the greater part of them [Q. the burghers?] took pity, for they knew that the young wise king and his people were wronged, and they did not wish to have the guilt of his blood on them, and they helped the young wise king and his companions to regain their liberty; but they were fed very scantily, and during a long time.

*Gerard de Roo's Version of Maximilian's Wedding.**

Frederick was well informed of all these matters, and sent the Bishop of Mayence, Louis Duke of Bavaria, and George Hesler † ambassadors to Brussels, with orders to wait there till sent for by Mary to Ghent. The Duke of Cleves endeavoured to induce them to return home, but without success. Others in the interests of Maximilian, and chiefly Madame Hallewin and the widow of Charles, advised them to proceed to Ghent.

They were received in the hall where the council was

* Librarian to Archduke Ferdinand of Austria: "Annales Rerum Belli Domique ab Austriacis Habspurgicæ Gentibus." Edited after Roo's death by Conrad Decius (a Meydenberg), Secretary to his Highness. Innspruck, 1592.
† Said by Molinet to be a very elegant prothonotary.—ED.

assembled, and Mary presided. She acknowledged that she had, at the request of her father, betrothed herself to Maximilian, sending letters and a ring to him, and added that she should carry out her obligations. The council admired her resolution, and Cleves, in great anger, returned home. The legates next proceeded to Louvain, and attended a convention, which confirmed the arrangements determined on at Ghent, and they then, having so happily discharged their duties, returned home. Louis, furious at the frustration of his plans, invaded and took possession of Artois.

"At the close of June the arrival of Maximilian at Cologne was announced. His retinue consisted, according to Commines, of eight hundred horse ; among whom were John, the Elector of Trèves ; Albert of Brandenburg ; Christopher of Baden ; William, the Prince of Julia ; and many equestrian nobles, all dressed-in mourning clothes. Mary in the mean time, having celebrated solemn funeral rites in honour of her father, ordered that such preparations as were due to his rank should be made to receive Maximilian and his followers.

"As soon as the young archduke had heard that the funeral rites of Charles had been performed, he changed his dress, and led his Germans, remarkable for the splendour of their dresses and gold decorations, and for the tallness of their figures and graceful horsemanship.

"In company with Maximilian was Charles Chymaius, who, taken prisoner at Nancy, had been liberated and led to Germany. When he came into the hall, meeting Mary, his betrothed, he saluted and embraced her ; and she, shedding tears of joy, testified her affection for him. Then each returned to their allotted quarters. On the 18th of August, 1477, being as soon as arrangements could be made, the nuptials were celebrated, the Bishop of Tornach being the officiating priest ; and among others present was Cardinal Julian, the pontifical legate. After the service they had feasts, dances, and knightly games, in which, it is related, the Germans displayed themselves excellently, their prince having accustomed them to their use."

HANS BURGMAIR, DESIGNER OF THE TRIUMPH.

Hans Burgmair the elder was the son of a painter,
Thomas Burgmair, and was born at Augsburg in 1473.

Of the events of his life but little is known with certainty
beyond the dates of his birth and death. It has been
asserted that he became the pupil of Martin Schongauer,
of Colmar, in 1488; and if the evidence in favour of
this opinion is slight, yet there is no evidence of any kind
to the contrary. Passavant, in his " Peintre Graveur," has
collected all that is known with regard to Burgmair, and
he gives (vol. ii. p. 103) the facts which seem to favour this
theory. He describes an ancient writing found at the back
of the Munich portrait of Schongauer, which contains the
autograph of Hans Largkmair or Burgkmair, describing
himself as Schongauer's pupil, and states that the characters
have much analogy with the known signatures of Burgmair, except the initial letter. Passavant also cites the
wood-engraving of the Virgin and Child, Bartsch, No. 13,
which has, he says, a great analogy with the manner of
Schongauer. The writing containing the autograph is reproduced in Bartsch, vol. vi. plate 1.; but Passavant states
that it is not copied with sufficient accuracy to make it of
value for reference. Whoever was his master, he soon fell
under the influence of Albert Durer, although there is no
reason for believing that he ever studied under him.

·The portrait of Burgmair and his wife, painted by himself, preserved in the Belvedere Gallery at Vienna, gives
his wife's age as fifty-two, and his as fifty-six, in 1528,
which accords with the date of his birth, 1473. Bartsch
gives the date of this picture as 1529, which would require
him to have been born in 1474; but he states also that he
was born in 1473.

It appears, from the record book of Painters (Gerech-
tigkeitsbuch), that Burgmair was dead in 1531; he must
therefore have died between 1528 and 1531; and it is not
possible to find the date with greater precision, as his son,
Hans Burgmair the younger, who drew in a similar manner,
used the same mark. It is impossible to separate the

designs of the father and the son, except in such cases as those of the Wise King and of the Triumphs; and it seems not improbable that the son should in these have assisted his father. Passavant attributes all the etchings on metal to Burgmair the younger, including the Venus and Mercury, Bartsch, No. 1, and bases his opinion on a comparison of the plate with the etching of the arms of Augsburg and others dated 1545, and he adds more conclusively, that the style proves it to belong to a period subsequent to the death of the father. Burgmair the younger was still living in 1559, as appears from a letter from the Emperor Ferdinand I. to the Council of Augsburg, and was at that time employed to etch on iron armour (Passavant, vol. iii. p. 266). It is almost certain that the elder Burgmair never engraved on wood himself, as in the instances in which the circumstances of the production of the blocks are known they were cut by other hands. The correspondence of Peutinger with the Emperor, brought out in 1851 by Theodore Herberger, and quoted by Passavant, throws considerable light upon the practice of the art of engraving at that time; and from various passages it may be inferred, with almost absolute certainty, that few among the painters and designers, and those men of less importance and consideration, such as Altdorfer, cut the blocks with their own hands. It seems probable also that the practice, not uncommon in our own day, of the drawing being made on the wood by an artist other than the designer, was then sometimes followed, since the letter of Dienecker of the 20th of October, 1512, contains this passage : " I shall be ready to prepare all work for the cutters, and will afterwards finish and polish it with my own hands, in order that the work and piecework should be all alike in the cut, and finished all by the same hand, so that nobody would doubt it." Dienecker here proposes to prepare the work; by which he probably means to draw the design upon the block.

If we except Albert Durer and Hans Holbein, the paintings of German artists are not much sought for or known in this country. Dr. Dibdin is not a high authority in art; but he was a shrewd observer, and a good listener when necessary. He (" Antiquarian Tour," vol. iii. p. 85), speak_ ing of the Augsburg Picture Gallery, says, " I shall now give you a notion of the talent of Hans Burgmair, a painter, as well as *engraver*, of first-rate abilities. I will begin with what I consider the most elaborate specimen of his pencil in this most curious gallery of pictures. The subject is serious, but miscellaneous, and of the date of 1501. It consists of patriarchs, evangelists, martyrs, male and female, and Popes, &c. The Virgin and Child are sitting above, in distinguished mazes, &c.

" The countenances of the whole group are full of nature and expression : that of the Virgin is doubtless painted after a living subject. It exhibits the prevailing or favourite mouth of the artist, which happens, however, to be generally somewhat awry. The cherub, holding up a white crown, and thrusting his arm, as it were, towards the spot where it is to be fixed, is prettily conceived. . . . . This picture contains some very fine heads. Another picture of Hans Burgmair worth especial attention is dated 1504. It is, as usual, divided into three compartments, the subject, St. Ursula and her virgins. Though of less solid merit than the preceding, it is infinitely more striking, being most singularly conceived and executed. The gold ornaments and gold grounds are throughout managed with a freedom and minuteness of touch which distinguish many of the most beautiful early missals. In the first compartment, or division, is a group of women round ' *Sibila Ancyra Phrygiæ.*' The dresses of these women, especially about the breast, are very curious. Some of their head-dresses are not less striking, but more simple, having what may be called a cushion of gold at the back of them. In the second compartment is the *Crucifixion* in the warmest and richest (says my memorandum, taken on the spot) glow of colour. Beneath there is a singular composition. Before a church is a group of pilgrims with staves and hats on ; a man not in the attire of a pilgrim heads them ; he is habited in green, and points backwards towards a woman, who is retreating ; a book in his left hand. Further to the right a man is retreating, going through an archway with a badge (a pair of cross-keys) on his shoulder. The retreating woman has also the same badge. To the left another pilgrim is sitting, apparently to watch ; further up is a house, towards which all the pilgrims seem to be directing their steps to enter. A man and a woman come out of this house to receive them with open arms. The third division continues the history of St. Ursula. Her attire is sumptuous in the extreme ; she sits in a vessel beside her husband Gutherus. A Pope and Cardinal are to the right of St. Ursula, the whole being a perfect blaze of splendour. Below they are dragging the female saint and her virgin companions on shore for the purpose of decapitation. An attitude of horror in one of the virgins is very striking.

"There is a small picture by Burgmair of the *Virgin and Christ*, in the manner of the Italian masters, which is a palpable failure. The infant is wretchedly drawn, although prettily and tenderly coloured. Burgmair was out of his element in subjects of *repose*. Where the workings of the mind were not to be depicted by strong demarcations of countenance, he was generally unsuccessful. Hence it is that in a subject of the greatest repose, but at the same time intensity of feeling—the *Crucifixion*—this master, in a picture here, of the date of 1519, has really outdone himself, and perhaps is not to be excelled by *any* artist of the same period. It is thus treated : Our Saviour has just breathed His dying exclamation, 'It is finished.' His head hangs down, cold, pale death being imprinted upon every feature of the face. It is, perhaps, a painfully-deadly countenance, copied, I make no doubt, from nature. St. Anne, Mary, and St. John are the only attendants. The first is quite absorbed in agony ; her head is lowly inclined, and her arms are above it. The pattern of the drapery is rather singular. Mary exhibits a more quiet expression ; her resignation is calm and fixed, while her heart seems to be broken. But it is in the figure and countenance of *St. John* that the artist has reached all that an artist could reach in a delineation of the same subject. The beloved disciple simply looks upwards upon the breathless corpse of his crucified master. In that look the world appears to be for ever forgotten. His arms and hands are locked together in the

K

agony of his soul. There is the sublimest abstraction from every artificial and frivolous accompaniment in the treatment of this subject which you can possibly conceive. The background of the picture is worthy of its nobler parts. There is a sobriety of colouring abouf it which Annibal Carracci would not have disdained to own. I should add that there is a folding compartment on each side of the principal subject, which, moving upon hinges, may be turned inwards, and shut out the whole from view : each of these compartments contains one of the two thieves who were crucified with our Saviour. There is a figure of St. Lazarus below one of them, which is very fine in colour and drawing."

The Editor has ventured to correct a few words in Dr. Dibdin's description of Burgmair's triptychs, for the sake of the grammar.

THE ENGRAVERS OF THE TRIUMPH.

HANS LEONARD SCHAUFELEIN, who held a distinguished position in art during the first half of the sixteenth century, was the son of a rich merchant of Nordlingen, François Schaufelein. The date of the painter's birth is unknown, but is supposed to have been about 1490. It probably was earlier, as in 1507 his name occurs in connection with a book entitled " Speculum Passionis," published by Ulrich Pinder, and printed at Nuremberg in 1507. It was illustrated by Schaufelein with thirty-seven woodcuts. He became the pupil of Durer, and afterwards remained as companion ; when he went, and the length of his apprenticeship, are unknown, but it is known that he left him in 1512. The usual custom in those times was for a pupil to remain five years, and not till after the expiration of that time could he work on his own account. In 1512 he went to Augsburg to illustrate the Thuerdanck, a

romantic poem, supposed to have been written by Maximilian I., to illustrate his exploits in peace and war, and
his marriage. The cuts were designed by Schaufelein, and
numbered 118, eight of which, says Bartsch, are signed by
Schaufelein. Passavant says two only are signed ; but if
the little shovel belongs to Schaufelein, then there are
three, Nos. 48, 69, and 70, the last-mentioned having no
monogram. No. 30 has a mark which is not Schaufelein's.
Bartsch gives the following description of the size of the cuts:
height, $5\frac{10-11}{12}$ in.; width, $4\frac{11}{12}$ in. Passavant does not correct
this error. The size is, height, $6\frac{8}{12}$ in. ; width, $5\frac{6}{12}$ in. Many
of the cuts are singularly bad. Some twenty are of superior
workmanship, but all are deficient in perspective. It appears
that Maximilian saw them before they were published, and
one can only wonder that he sanctioned such grotesque
illustrations of his adventures, as most of them render him
ridiculous.

He quarrelled with Schonsperger, the printer of the
Thuerdanck, and left Augsburg.

Between this time and 1515 he is traced by his paintings, executing a fine altar-piece in the abbey of the
Benedictines at Anhausen, near Oettingen, and in 1515 he
was made a burgher of Nordlingen for a large picture of
the siege of Bethulia.

In 1516 he married Afra Tucher, and settled at Nordlingen. He died in 1540, having led a tranquil but labo-
rious life, as the number of his works testifies. As to their
character, we may quote the words of Dr. Waagen, in his
"Manuel de l'Histoire de la Peinture," Stuttgart, 1862, in
8vo. : " Schaufelein adhered faithfully to the manner of
Durer. He possessed a power of invention more rich than
profound, especially capable of rendering lively and ani-
mated actions. One finds at the same time in him an
ardent and profound sensibility, a very distinct feeling for
beauty of form, grace in action, and of purity of taste in
the arrangement of .draperies and costumes. For colour
and method of handling the brush, the works of the old
painter Frederick Herlen had evidently been carefully

studied by him. The tone of his colour is rather warmer and more harmonious than Durer's."

The work which best sustains Schaufelein's reputation out of Germany is " Les Danseurs des Noces " (Bartsch, " Peintre Graveur," vol. vii. No. 103). This author had apparently not seen the complete work. No. 96, which constitutes the twenty-first and last cut of the Danseurs, is there described by him as a separate piece. Bartsch is also in error as to the size of the figures. There is no border, and the measurement must be made from the head to the foot, except where a little foreground is found. Of the twenty cuts which he recognizes as the work, he gives the dimensions as 8 inches $\frac{6}{12}$ lines. They should be described as varying in height from about 8 to above 10 inches; the dimensions of the twenty-first cut as, width 15 inches, height 10 inches. It should be, width 16 inches 3 lines, height 10 inches 10 to 11 lines. Passavant, in his observations on Bartsch's notice of Schaufelein's works, does not notice this.

JEROME ANDRE.—Von Murr, who has been followed by most of the authorities upon the subject, has, on the authority of Neudoerffer, given as his real name Jerome Resch. There is, however, in the cemetery of St. John a tomb, mentioned by Passavant, vol. i. page 75, note, of Jeronymus Andre, formschneider, with the date of his death, May 7, 1556. It would seem not improbable from this that Jerome Andre was not the same as Jerome Resch. Neudoerffer of Nuremberg, who wrote in 1546, relates of Jerome of Nuremberg, or Jerome Resch, that he lived in that town, and engraved most of the woodcuts of Albert Durer, and among others the Triumphal Car, during the progress of which work the Emperor visited him almost daily. He speaks of him as the most able woodcutter of his day.

WILHELM and CORNELIS LIEFRINK lived at Augsburg, and engraved designs of both Burgmair and Durer.

HANS LIEFRINK was probably the same who is known by some engravings both on wood and metal, and who lived at Antwerp from 1540 to 1580. He is said to have belonged originally to Leyden, and was probably a member of the same family as Cornelis and Wilhelm Liefrink mentioned above. Passavant describes a fine wood-engraving of Duke William of Juliers and Cleves, inscribed, "Hans Liefrink formschnyder," in the collection at Amsterdam.

JOST DIENECKER, or DE NEGKER, originally of Antwerp, established himself at Augsburg about 1510. He never appears as a designer, but his talent and ability entitle him to be called an artist with Jerome of Nuremberg, and Hans Lutzelburger of Basle. In his letters of the 20th and 27th October, 1512, sent to the Emperor Maximilian, it appears that other engravers were employed to assist him in the production of his woodcuts for the Emperor, but that he finished each block himself, so that it could not be seen that more than one hand had been employed. He seems to claim also to have invented the method of producing chiaroscuros with three wood blocks, and refers to the portrait of Hans Baumgartner, engraved on three blocks after Burgmair. This engraving is dated 1512; but there is an earlier one designed by Burgmair of a woman flying from death (Bartsch, 40), of which Passavant gives additional particulars. It bears the date 1510, and one copy in the Albertine collection has the name of Jost de Negker inscribed. There is also an engraving of Hans Baldung Grun of sorcerers (Bartsch, 55), from three blocks; but this may have been engraved after Dienecker's was produced, or it may have been engraved by him from the design of Baldung Grun. To Lucas Cranach, however, belongs the credit of first producing chiaro-scuro engravings, as some of his, but printed from two blocks only, are dated as early as 1506. Dienecker probably means to claim, in his letter to the Emperor, not the original invention, but the improvement of the process. The date of his death is not known, but took place before 1561, as in that year David de Negker,

wood-engraver, of Augsburg, and probably his son, repub-
lished under his own name Dienecker's copies of Holbein's
Dance of Death, which were brought out first in 1544.

He usually marked pieces engraved by him with his
name, sometimes spelt one way, and sometimes the other;
but on one piece (Bartsch, No. 25 in Burgmair's works) he
used a monogram.

CATALOGUE OF THE WORKS OF BURGMAIR.

Bartsch's "Peintre-Graveur," vol. vii. p. 197.

ETCHING.

1. VENUS AND MERCURY.

At the right, Venus standing, holding an arrow in the left hand, endeavouring with the right hand to awaken Mercury, who sleeps, sitting near a fountain at the foot of a palm-tree. To the right, in the air, is Cupid. A bandrol, with the letters H B, is placed at the foot, on the same side. This plate, etched with acid on iron, is the only print which Burgmair ever engraved.

Height 6 inches 8 lines, width 4 inches 9 lines.

See Passavant, "Etchings of Burgmair the Younger." *

WOOD ENGRAVINGS.

OLD TESTAMENT.

1. Eve persuading Adam to eat the forbidden Fruit. Eve is standing to the left, and Adam to the right, of the engraving. In the distance, to the left, God is represented creating Eve during the sleep of Adam. On the lower margin we find this inscription: " Und Got Gesegnet sy . . . unnder dem hi Gen. am j."

A large piece of eight plates joined together.

Height 33 inches 2 lines, width 24 inches.

This work is indifferently drawn and badly cut.

---

* Passavant's observations on, and additions to, Bartsch are given, by permission of the publishers, at the end of this list.

2. Samson killing the Lion. The letters H B are engraved on a quiver, towards the top, on left.

Height 4 inches 3 lines, width 3 inches.

3. Pharaoh drowned in the Red Sea pursuing the people of Israel. Marked H B, below, at the left, in white.

Height 6 inches 5 lines, width 4 inches 6 lines.

This piece, and the engravings under the numbers 16, 62, and 71, are to be found in a collection of sermons by Gayler of Kaysersperg, printed at Augsburg in 1510, by H. Otmar. In folio.

4. Solomon adoring an Idol. Marked H B, at the right.

Height 4 inches 5 lines, width 3 inches 6 lines.

5. Bathsheba in the Bath. Marked H B, below, at right, and dated at the top, 1519. Same size.

6. Dalilah cutting off Samson's hair. Marked below, at right.

Same size.

We sometimes find these three last printed in a passe-partout, an architectural border adorned with vases, dolphins, fantastical animals, &c. This passe-partout is 8 inches in height and 5 inches 8 lines in width.

NEW TESTAMENT.

7. The Virgin seated, holding a book in the right hand, the other supporting the infant Jesus on her knees. Marked on a bandrol at right top.

Height 8 inches 3 lines, width 5 inches 7 lines.

This engraving is sometimes met with enclosed in a passepartout, presenting an architectural border. This passe-partout is 11 inches 7 lines in height and 8 inches in width.

8. The Virgin with the Infant Jesus in her Arms. Marked, and dated 1518, at left top.

This is hardly more than an engraving in outline.

Height 8 inches 9 lines, width 6 inches 1 line.

9. The Virgin seated, and turned to the right. She watches the infant Jesus on her knees, and holds his right foot. Marked H B on a table, at right.

Height 8 inches 9 lines, width 6 inches 6 lines.

10. The same piece engraved a second time, with many alterations. The principal consists of the addition of the words, "Pater noster," &c., written in the open book, which is placed on a stone. Marked in the same way. It is better drawn, and the cutting is more delicate than the last.

Height 8 inches 9 lines, width 7 inches 7 lines.

11. The same, engraved a third time, without the initials. In the margin below, the "Salve Regina," in German, is printed with *movable type* (?). Below we read, "Jost de Negker zu Augsburg," apparently the name of the engraver.

Height 7 inches 7 lines, width 5 inches 4 lines.

12. The same, engraved a fourth time, "Pater noster," &c., is inscribed on the book. The H of the mark is without the horizontal line. In a bandrol at the base of the engraving we read, "O Mater Dei, memento mei."

Height 8 inches 8 lines, width 7 inches 4 lines.

13. The Virgin seated, and turned to the left. Her right hand on the knee of the infant Jesus; with her left she presents him an apple. A bandrol; with the letters H B below, at right. On left, a château with a balcony.

Height 8 inches, width 5 inches 11 lines.

14. Jesus Christ driving the Sellers out of the Temple. Marked at bottom H B.

Height 3 inches 4 lines, width 2 inches 5 lines.

This piece is found in a work entitled "Das Leiden Jesu Christi, &c., Durch Wolfgang von Mann in Gesatzweise bezwungen. Augsp. 1515. Bey dem jungen Hans Schönsperger." 4to. It is surrounded by a passe-partout 5 inches 3 lines high and 3 inches 6 lines wide.

(*See Passavant's Observations.*)

L.

15. The Resurrection of Lazarus. Marked, at right, bottom.

Height 5 inches 3 lines, width 3 inches 5 lines.

Found in the same work as the last.

16. Jesus Christ, Lazarus, Martha, Mary, and the Magdalen. In the middle of the engraving, Jesus Christ, seated, listens to Martha talking. She is standing on his right hand; Mary, on her knees, to the left; and near her, Lazarus standing. Mark, in middle, at top, on a mantelpiece.

Height 6 inches 3 lines, width 4 inches 6 lines.

17. Jesus Christ at the Mount of Olives. He is represented on his knees praying and turned to the left. Three of his disciples sleep on the ground in front. In the distance is Judas, at the head of a troop of Jewish soldiers, who come to seize Christ. Below we read, "O Herr Jésu christe . . . . deinem gotlichen willen." Marked at right, bottom, and dated 1524, in a cartouche in margin. A large plate of four pieces joined. It is poorly designed and badly engraved, as also is the following engraving, No. 19.

Height 32 inches 8 lines, width 24 inches. The lower margin three inches deep.

18. Jesus Christ on the Cross, between the two Thieves. Below, John and the three Marys. Marked below, in middle.

Height 5 inches 2 lines, width 3 inches 5 lines.

This is found in the work of Wolfgang von Mann, mentioned at No. 14.

19. Jesus on the Cross, between the two Thieves. At the foot of the Cross, on the left, is the Virgin and St. John and four female Saints; on the right, four men, one of whom carries a cloak and pincers. Marked below, in middle. On the lower margin is written, "Herr Jesu Christe, der du . . . . meins tods beuolhen sein." Dated 1526, in a cartouche in margin. A large piece of eight plates joined together.

Height 32 inches, width 24 inches.

20. The Bust of the Saviour, seen in profile in a medallion. Inscription, "Tu es Christus filius," &c. There is above an accompanying text describing the discovery of the medallion, and below, an epistle of Lentulus, which treats of the expression of the features of Christ. Marked, in middle, at bottom.

Diameter of the medallion 4 inches 1 line.

21. The Bust of the Saviour, seen in profile and turned to the left. In a medallion. Marked on a tablet at right.

Height and width 8 inches 6 lines.

22. Head of Christ, full face, and crowned with thorns. The Sudary forms the background. Marked H B, at right, in margin below.

Height 7 inches, width 5 inches 7 lines.

Proofs are occasionally seen with this inscription on the margin, " Salve scta facies nostri redeptooris." There are also proofs with St. Veronica holding the sudary. This figure is half-length, and engraved on another block joined to the preceding, giving the appearance of a single engraving.

Later proofs of this piece have a monogram composed of the letters H L, indicating the engraver. Burgmair's initials absent. Height 5 inches 7 lines, width 3 inches 10 lines.

MALE AND FEMALE SAINTS.

23. St. George on horseback, turned to the right. This inscription is on the left, above: "Divus Georgius Christianorum militum propugnator." Below we have "H BURGK-MAIR." A very fine work.

Height 12 inches, width 8 inches 7 lines.

We find the first proofs of this engraving in chiaroscuro, done with two blocks. Below, at right, signed Jost de Negker. These names were removed from the after-copies.

24. St. Luke painting the Portrait of the Virgin, who is seated under a portico. In the middle, towards the bottom, is the mark, and towards the top the date, 1507.

Height 8 inches 2 lines, width 5 inches 6 lines.

25. St. Sebastian fastened to a Column in the midst of an Arcade. Towards the bottom, at left, is the date 1512, and at right, "H BURGMAIR." It also has the monogram of Josse de Negker. The engraving is arched above.

Height 5 inches 6 lines, width 2 inches 8 lines.

St. Sebastian is placed in a niche, which is a passe-partout of 7 inches 10 lines in height, and 5 inches 8 lines in width.

26. St. Anne receiving the Infant Jesus from the hands of the Holy Virgin. The former is accompanied by St. Joachim, the latter by St. Joseph. At bottom, at right, is a bandrol marked H B, and dated 1512.

Height 8 inches 3 lines, width 5 inches 7 lines.

27. St. Clara standing. No mark.

Height 6 inches, width 2 inches 9 lines.

This Saint is placed in a niche, a passe-partout, the same as is used in No. 25, in the first impressions of Nos. 48—54 and 55—61. This seems a proof that this piece was engraved after a design by Burgmair, and it follows as a fair induction that all these were engraved by De Negker, as they are all finished in the same style as this No. 27, which bears the name of that engraver in a tablet below.

28. St. Elizabeth represented Spinning. She is in the centre of the engraving, and turned towards the right. Five women occupied in spinning surround her. The name S. ELSBETH is inscribed on a bandrol above. Low down on the left is a shield with a lion rampant. Below the shield is a mark, which is open to doubt whether it means Burgmair or some other artist, since it differs from the mark by which Burgmair is constantly known.

Height 6 inches 4 lines, width 5 inches.

This engraving is to be found in a work of Hans Gayler, of Kaisersperg, entitled, "Das Buch Granatapfel." Folio.

(See Passavant's Observations.)

29. St. Radian attacked by two Wolves. Marked H B at left, low, on a square stone. Very fine.

Height 5 inches, width 3 inches 9 lines.

30. The same, treated differently. On the right, a cardinal is on his knees praying. Marked H B at bottom, at left. A fine piece.

    Height 4 inches 10 lines, width 3 inches 6 lines.

31. The same, treated differently. Marked H B at bottom, at left.

    Height 7 inches 8 lines, width 5 inches 9 lines.

PORTRAITS.

32. The Emperor Maximilian I. in complete armour, on horseback, and turned to the left. Above we read, "Imp. Cæs. Maximil. Aug.," and below the date, 1518, "H BURGKMAIR."

    Height 12 inches, width 8 inches 5 lines.

There are proofs of this in chiaroscuro in two blocks, which are rare.

33. Bust of Pope Julius II. in a medallion. Dated 1511, towards the bottom, at left ; and below that is a tablet inscribed "H BURGKMAIR."

    Height and width 9 inches 2 lines.

    (*See Passavant's Observations.*)

34. Jean Paungartner, a member of the Imperial Council. Half-length. Three-quarter face, turned to the left. Inscribed, in a tablet at top, at right, "AN. SAL. MDXII. IOANNES PAVNGARTNER C. AVGVSTA. AETAT. SVAE. LVII." In the middle of the left, marked "H BURGKMAIR."

This is a chef-d'œuvre of wood-engraving, executed in chiaroscuro, on two blocks. It has a rare finish.

    Height 10 inches 10 lines, width 9 inches.

    (*See Passavant's Observations.*)

ARMS.

35. The Imperial double Eagle, accompanied by three emblazoned shields, protected by the wings. Above the shield, on the left, we read, "Ingoldstadium, 1473;" in the centre, "Friburgum, 1462;" on the right, "Tibinga, 1478." Above is written, "Tibi gloria semper." Marked below H B. A medallion.

Height and width 4 inches 9 lines.

36. Five Shields on the same block. The first, at top, at left, a double imperial eagle; the second, a single eagle; the third, in the centre, contains five lions and griffins rampant; the fourth, below, at left, an ass; the fifth, a boar's head. Marked H B at bottom, in middle.

Height 6 inches 9 lines, width 5 inches 3 lines.

37. Unknown Arms. The shield is quarterly. First, two leopards. Second, semé of hearts, a lion rampant. Third, a lion rampant. Fourth, a lion rampant, within a bordure compony. The crest consists of a horse without furniture, near a column planted between two sickles, adorned with eyes from the peacock's tail. Marked H B below, in the middle.

Height 7 inches 9 lines, width 6 inches.

38. The Arms of George Baron of Limburg, Bishop of Bamberg, who died in 1522. The shield is quarterly. First and fourth, a lion rampant charged with a bend. Second, three points (?). Third, five shovels. The shield is surmounted by a bishop's mitre.

Height 6 inches, width 4 inches 3 lines.

No initials, but it is generally considered to be by Burgmair.

ALLEGORICAL SUBJECTS.

39. An Allegorical piece, forming the frontispiece of a book. Above is written: "Dyalogus Johannis Stamler Augustin. de diversarum gentium sectis et mundi religionibus." Low on the right there is a tablet with the letters H B.

The execution is inferior.

Height 10 inches 7 lines, width 6 inches 10 lines.

40. A Young Woman shrieking and flying from Death, who is
pitilessly killing a Young Man.   In chiaroscuro, from three
blocks.   Marked at bottom, on left, " H BURGK-
MAIR." A fine piece.

Height 7 inches 10 lines, width 5 inches 8 lines.

(*See Passavant's Observations.*)

41—47. The Seven Planets. A set of seven engravings. They
are represented by the fabulous gods and goddesses,
standing in architectural niches.   Above each figure is
inscribed, in Roman capitals, the name of the divinity ;
thus, SATVRNVS, IVBITER, &c.   In a tablet on
the pedestal of each figure is the mark H B.

The height of each figure is about $5\frac{1}{2}$ inches.

The same passe-partout, 11 inches 2 lines in height and 6 inches
11 lines wide, surrounds each figure and forms the niche.

48—54. The Seven Cardinal Virtues.   A set of seven plates.
They are represented by female figures standing in architectural niches.   Above each figure, in capital letters, the
name of each virtue is given ; thus,—

DER GLAVB	DIE STERCK
HOFFNVNG	DIE GERECHTIGKAIT
DIE LIEBE	DIE FIRSICHTIKAIT
DIE MESIKAIT	

The same passe-partout serves for all seven, and forms the
niche. It is a copy of that of No. 25. Marked H B at bottom.
The figures are poorly drawn and coarsely cut.

Height 8 inches, width 5 inches 9 lines.

There are three different proofs of this set. The first, that
above described. In the second, the figures are in the same
niche, but there is besides a border composed of four longish
plates filled with foliage. The top one contains two medallions
with busts, and the bottom one a cartouche, containing the name
of the virtue, printed with type. This set, with both passe-par-
touts, is $11\frac{1}{4}$ inches high and $7\frac{1}{4}$ inches wide.

The third exhibits the figures alone, without niches or borders.

Height about 6 inches, width about 2 inches 8 lines.

55—61. The Seven Mortal Sins. Set of seven engravings. The sins are represented by standing figures in architectural niches. Above each figure the name of the sin is written in German, with roman capitals :—

DIE HOFART   DIE FRESIKAIT
DIE GEITIKAIT   DER NEID
VNKEISCH   DIE TRAKAIT
DER ZORN

Height 6 inches, width 2 inches 9 lines.

A passe-partout, used for each of the seven, forms the niche. In the middle of the base are the letters H B on a scroll. The passe-partout is 11 inches in height by 7 inches in width.

This series is met with without a passe-partout.

62. Seven Demons, represented by very hideous chimerical animals, armed with a sabre ; on the blade of each is expressed, in German, the names of the mortal sins. Marked H B at bottom, at right.

Height 6 inches 4 lines, width 4 inches 6 lines.

MISCELLANEOUS.

63. Alboinus, King of the Lombards, and Athanaric, King, or rather Judge, of the Goths, seated opposite to each other, conversing. Marked H B at top, at right. Very well engraved. It has served as a frontispiece to a book, entitled "Jornandes de Rebus Gothorum, &c. Aug. Vindel. Per Jo. Miller, 1515." Folio.

64—69. The Three Good Men and Women of the Christians, of the Jews, and of the Pagans. Set of six engravings.

Height 7 inches 2 lines, width 4 inches 9 lines.

(64.) Charlemagne, Godfrey of Burgundy, and King Arthur. Marked H B at bottom, at right.

(65.) St. Helena, St. Bridget, and St. Elizabeth. Marked H B at bottom, at left.

(66.) Joshua, David, and Judas Maccabeus. Marked H B at bottom, at left.

(67.) Esther, Judith, Jael. Marked H B at bottom, at left.

(68.) Hector, Alexander the Great, and Julius Cæsar. Marked H B at bottom, at right.

(69.) Lucretia, Veturia, and Virginia. Marked H B, and dated 1519 in the middle, at the bottom.

These six plates were engraved by Jost de Negker, who adds his name, thus, "Jost de Negker zu Augspurg," at the bottom of No. 64, and of 67 in a small separate plate.

This series is met with in three states.

The first as described.

The second are enclosed in a passe-partout representing a portico, the pediment enriched with two figures holding a cartouche. The cartouche is blank.

Height 11 inches 10 lines, width 8 inches.

The third are the same as the second, with the addition of four German verses printed with type in each cartouche.

70. A Man speaking to a King seated on a Throne. Marked H B at left, top.

Height 6 inches, width 5 inches.

71. A Cook drawing a Hare, hanging from a wall on the right. The distance shows a kitchen with a fireplace, below which, towards the left, is the mark H B.

Height 6 inches 4 lines, width 4 inches 6 lines.

This piece has also been engraved, and with a better result, from a drawing by Hans Baldung Grün. (Bartsch, No. 47 in Grün's works.)

72. Two Pilgrims directing their Steps, towards the right of the engraving. They are followed by a woman who leads a child by the hand. The mark H B is engraved on the right, at the base of a cruciform sepulchre-stone at the foot of a tree.

Height 7 inches, width 5 inches 2 lines.

This piece is found in the Sermons of Jean de Kaisersperg. Strasburg, 1508, published by Hans Otmar. Folio.

M

73. A Woman on the Back of a Man, who crawls on all-fours. Marked H B in middle, at bottom.

Height 4 inches 4 lines, width 3 inches 6 lines.

74. Six Doctors seated round a Table. The centre figure seems to explain to the others the text of a large book, open before him. Marked H B at right, at bottom.

Height 5 inches 5 lines, width 4 inches 5 lines.

This piece has been employed at page 78 of a German translation of the Offices of Cicero. Augsburg, 1545, by H. Steiner. Fol. min.

75. A Savage standing at the right, presenting a bunch of herbs to a female savage carrying a baby on her left arm and holding a stick in her right hand. Both are clothed in the skins of panthers. High up on the left we read, "IN ALLAGO." Marked H B on a stone at the right, low. An indifferent engraving.

Height 8 inches 6 lines, width 5 inches 8 lines.

76. A Rhinoceros seen in profile. High up on the left we read, "*Rhinoceros*, M.D.XV. Marked H B on a bandrol low on the right.

Height 11 inches 8 lines, width 7 inches 10 lines.

77. The King of Gutzin carried on a Litter by four savages, and preceded and followed by a dozen more of his Subjects, some playing on different Instruments, the others carrying Arms. The procession is advancing to the right. Above we read, "DER KVNIG VON GVTZIN." Above, on the left, in a tablet, is the mark H B, and date, 1508. Four plates joined in width.

Height 9 inches 10 lines, width 47 inches 8 lines.

(*See Passavant's Observations.*)

78. Nine different Pommels of Swords, in three rows of three pieces. On the margin below is written, "Gedruckt zu Augspurg durch Jobst de Necker Fürmschneider." It is probable that Jost de Necker engraved these from Burgmair's designs.

Height 12 inches 6 lines, width about 8 inches 4 lines.

SERIES OF ENGRAVINGS.

79. The Genealogy of the Emperor Maximilian I. A set of
77 engravings, each with a separate figure. Each prince
is represented in full armour, with an escutcheon beside
him. Some are standing, others sitting in varied attitudes.
Not having any bordures, it is difficult to state the size;
the standing figures are about six inches high. These
pieces are very rare. Each piece is marked H B.

(*See Passavant's Observations.*)

80. The Engravings for the work entitled "Weiss Kunig." A
series of 237 engravings, cut on wood by different engravers after designs by Burgmair.

This work was not completed during the lifetime of the
Emperor. It was published first in 1775, under this title:
"Der Weiss Kunig. Eine Erzählung von den Thaten Kaiser
Maximilian des ersten. Von Marx Treitzsaurwein auf dessen
Angeben zusammen getragen, &c. Herausgegeben aus dem
Manuscripte der k. k. Hofbibliothek Wien, auf Kosten Joseph
Kurzböcks, k. k. Hof buchdruckers." Folio. Twenty-four years
after J. Edwards, a London bookseller, having purchased the
remainders from the heirs of Kurzböck, replaced the German
text by a succinct explanation of the plates, written in French,
with this title: "Weiss Kunig. Tableau des principeaux évène-
mens de la vie et du règne de l'empereur Maximilien I. En
une suite de deux cent trente-sept planches gravées en bois sur
les desseins, et sous la conduite de Hans Burgmair. Imprimé à
Vienne, et se trouve à Londres chez J. Edwards. Pall-mall.
1799." All the engravings comprised in this work are 8 inches
2 lines in height, by 7 inches 2 to 3 lines in width; except
Nos. 156 and 199, which have 8 inches 10 lines in height and
7 inches 10 lines in width. The great diversity in the execution
of these prints proves that several engravers have been employed.
Only ninety-two* of these prints are marked H B. These are

---

* There is a mistake as to the size of the plates; 156 and 199 measure
h. 9 inches 4 lines, *w.* 8 inches 4 lines. There are 99 of the prints marked
H B.

No. 39 has the same monogram formed of the letters L B, as No. 78,
mentioned in the text.—ED.

the best, and it appears that Hans Burgmair himself drew the designs on the blocks.

The engraving No. 78 bears the monogram **⊞**. No. 199 bears the mark of Hans Springinklee. No. 200 has the mark of Hans Schäufelein. No. 237 is a modern engraving, cut at Vienna in 1775.

In the Court library at Vienna there is an ancient copy of this series of engravings, containing thirteen pieces, the wood blocks for which have disappeared, and which are absent in the edition of 1775. They are as follow :—

1. An old King with a large Beard, accompanied by a Queen, and followed by a great number of Court Ladies walking before the King, who stands on the right. In the distance, a chamber with two windows.

2. A Tournament with many Jousters. In the distance, spectators behind a barrier; and on the right, two trumpeters on horseback.

3. The Interior of a Church. On the left an altar, where a priest is administering the Lord's Supper to an old king. Behind, at the right, three saddled horses.

4. An old Prince under a Portico receiving the Deputies, two of whom have long plumes in their caps, which fall down their backs. In the distance, to the right, a saddled horse, secured by the bridle to the wall of a house. Marked H B on the pedestal of a column, low on the left.

5. A Battle. On the right, a company of infantry pursue the enemy, who retire fighting. Amongst the slain is a king with his crown on his head.

6. The Siege of a fortified place, which is seen in the distance. In the foreground is the camp of the Imperial troops, recognizable by the double eagle placed on the vane of the foremost tent to the left. This tent bears the mark H B.

7. Audience Hall. To the right a prince, followed by his ministers and some halberdiers. The prince is speaking to two men who stand opposite to him, one wearing a cap, and the other covered with a flat hat. In the centre of the distance is a throne, at the top of which is the mark H B.

8. Fight between two Bodies of Infantry. Those to the left have flags bearing a great cross, those to the right exhibiting the arms of Burgundy. At the head of the latter a halberdier is seen attacking a bowman.

9. The Assault of a Fortress. On the left of the foreground two tents, and six on the right. Marked H B on the nearest tent on the left.

10. Audience Hall. On the right, a young king speaks to four ministers, who surround him. In the left distance three lords are passing through a door accompanied by a herald.

11. The Interview of two Kings in an open Plain. They are on horseback, each accompanied by a detachment of cavalry. On the left foreground, a Turk on horseback. H B on a horse's breastplate, on the right.

12. A Battle. In front, a melee of cavaliers in full armour. Amongst the slain is a king lying on his back. In the middle distance a detachment of infantry pursue cavalry. In the distance, at the left, is a town; at the right, a camp. H B on the border of a horsecloth, in the middle of the foreground.

13. The original Engraving from which the copy was taken, which appears at No. 237 in the edition of 1776. Marked H B towards the right, in the foreground, on the border of a cloth.

(See Passavant's Observations.)

81. The Triumph.*

(See Passavant's Observations.)

82. Portraits of Saints belonging to the family of Maximilian. A series of 119 engravings by different hands.

Height 8 inches 8 lines, width 7 inches 8 lines.

This series was printed at Vienna in 1799. It is not known how far this series is complete. In the Imperial library at Vienna

---

* It is not necessary to give Bartsch's remarks on the " Triumph," as he merely copies without acknowledgment the French preface, of which, however, he may have been the author.—ED.

are 122 blocks; three of which, however, are so rotten as to be useless for printing purposes. The engravers are eight in number; Hans Frank, Cornelius Liefrink, Alexis Lindt, Josse de Negker, Wolfgang Resch, Hans Taberith, Wilhelm Taberith, Nikolaus Seemann.

These names, as well as the years 1515 and 1518, are traced in ink on most of the blocks. Excepting Wolfgang Resch and Nikolaus Seeman, these are the same as the engravers of the "Triumph of the Emperor Maximilian I.," No. 81. It is therefore almost certain that this series has been engraved after Burgmair, the rather that tradition has generally attributed to him the isolated prints that have been hitherto met with. Not one of them is marked H B.

In the Imperial library is to be seen an ancient copy of these engravings, probably printed during the Emperor's lifetime. It contains two cuts wanting in the new edition, the blocks having been lost. They are—

1. Saint Waudru, Abbess of Mons, in Hainault. She is in a hospital, giving her benediction to a poor lame man seated in front, to the left.

2. Saint Aldedrude, a daughter of Waudru. She is seen exorcising a young girl tied by ropes to a column.

HANS BURGMAIR (THE OLD AND THE YOUNG).

Passavant's "Peintre-Graveur," vol. iii. Schools of Augsburg and Bavaria, pp. 264—285.

WOOD ENGRAVINGS.

"Observations on Bartsch," vii. pp. 200—242.

Bathsheba at the Bath.
This is the only piece which is marked with the small h before the B.

14. The Passion of Jesus Christ (Das leiden Jesu Christi, &c. Augspurg, 1515).
In the book published by Wolfgang von Mann, with 30 wood engravings as large as the page, the first piece represents the author offering his book to the Emperor Maximilian ; it is without mark, it is true, but certainly belongs to Hans Burgmair, and is well executed.

28. St. Elizabeth.
This piece bears the monogram **HB** and from its appearance seems to have been engraved from a design by Hans Baldung Grun.

33. Julius II.
We find a chiaroscuro of two blocks, with the inscription, "Julius, Ligur Papa Secundus." A circular piece, $8\frac{9}{11}$ inches in diameter. Dresden.

34. Jean Paumgartner.
We find of this very fine piece, in chiaroscuro, copies printed with three blocks, and bearing the date 1512. We have already shown in our historical summary, by a letter addressed to the Emperor Maximilian, dated October 27, 1512, by Jost de Necker, that it was cut by this celebrated engraver.

40. A young Woman running away.

We find this again, with the date 1510, beside the name of Burgmair, and on a copy in the Albertine collection is seen, at the left of the pilaster, the name of Jost de Necker, which is the more interesting as showing that this distinguished wood engraver had already, in 1510, executed chiaroscuros with three blocks, and that he may claim the honour of being the inventor.

77. The King of Gutzin, 1508.

A second edition bears the date 1511. We also find a copy of four plates joined, with inscriptions. $h.$ 9$\frac{8}{13}$ in., $w.$ 46 in., of which there are recent prints in the Derschau collection, 11, No. 26.*

79. The Genealogy of the Emperor Maximilian.

This wood engraving was finished in 1510, as we learn from a letter of Peutinger in the same year, May 17, where, concerning this work and others of a similar kind which he had been commissioned by the Emperor to execute, he informs him that the engraver to whom he had confided the work had left Augsburg unknown to him, and that he must consequently look out for another artist to execute it (*ausmache*), and finishes with saying " that the painter here is well calculated for the work," a passage which we have already sought to explain in our historical dissertation and in the article on Hans Schaufelein. But this want of an engraver was soon satisfied, as Jost de Necker, of Antwerp, one of the most distinguished artists of this period and in this particular kind of work, settled in Augsburg the same year, as is proved by the date of the preceding piece, No. 40, " A young Woman," &c.

80. The Wise King.

Most of the engravings in this book were cut after designs by Burgmair, and these engravings bear his mark. One of them bears the monogram of Hans Schaufelein, **ĦSI** It is No. 200.

One other (No. 19†), that of Hans Springinklee, and others not

---

* The difference in the size of the blocks as given by Bartsch and Passavant indicates a copy.—ED.   † A mistake for 199.—ED.

signed, might equally have been designed by these artists, since they in no way resemble the manner of Burgmair, and want his breadth of composition. We may presume that this work was already commenced in 1511, from the date which we find attached to the initials on the gun in engraving 66, H. B. xi.*

The Imperial Library at Vienna possesses three proof-copies in the first state of nearly half of the 237 engravings which belong to this work ; viz. " Codex No. 3034. Question-book (Fragebuch) de 379 feuilles, large folio, dans laquel Max Treytzsaurwein alle mängl unnd fragstucke auff alle figuren vnnd schrifften, die in dem puch des weyssen kunigs begriffen sein, vnnd noch ju volendung desselben puechs darein gehören, in ditz puech geschrieben, dieselben mängl vnnd fragstuckh bey bemelter romischer kayserlicher maiestat zu erledigen. Sollich des Treytz-sauerweins einschreiben ist beschehen in den nechsten vierzehnde tagen nach pfingsten Anno vc in xv vnnd funffzehnenden pfing-sten (1515)." The 82 proofs have manuscript explanations. It contains three from the lost blocks :—1. The Coronation of the Emperor Frederick III. (B. No. 13), of which the copy is found in the edition of 1775, under the No. 237. 2. The Tourney (B. No. 2). 3. The Siege of a City (B. No. 6), which a manu-script note tells us is the siege of Padua. The 35 pen drawings found in the codex are inferior, and certainly do not belong to Burgmair.

Codex No. 3033. The land register-book, folio, containing 204 leaves and 155 engravings, in fine state, as in the first codex, but not always with a large margin, and some of them printed on the waste sheets of decrees of Maximilian I. of the 5th of October, 1514. It contains proofs of five of the lost blocks ; and on the funeral pomp of the Emperor Frederick, with the horses destined for sacrifice, we find written below with a pen, the name of " hans franck," probably that of the engraver, who is known as Hans Lutzelburger. We also find five middling pen drawings, like those of the preceding codex, and among others, that which has served for the lost block, No. 7, with this inscription, " der pes (böse) techant von genut " (the wicked Governor of Ghent).

Codex No. 3032 contains the fair copy of the text on 566 leaves, large folio, which is faithfully rendered in the edition of 1775. It is illustrated by 134 proofs from the blocks, but which are not

* This is probably not a date, but merely an ornament on the gun. Com-pare with this Plates 43 and 126. Plate 54 is dated 1515.—Ed.

as fine nor in as good preservation as those of the two preceding codices. Two of them are prints from the lost blocks; these are Nos. 2 and 13 in Bartsch.

The copy mentioned by Bartsch, vol. vii. p. 226, which was collected towards the middle of the sixteenth century (ex Bibl. Archiducis Ferdinandi), contains the twelve engravings (not thirteen) of which the blocks are lost. The block described by Bartsch under No. 4 as lost, is the No. 3 of the edition of 1775, and in this copy bears the inscription, " Excipit legator Bohemiæ et Ungariæ." A copy not mentioned by Bartsch (Cod. Ambras. 324) contains the impressions from the lost blocks Nos. 7 and 10. (See F. v. Bartsch, pp. 285—287.)

81. The Triumph of the Emperor Maximilian I. Series of 135 leaves.

An old copy in the library of the Emperor Ferdinand, before Archduke Ferdinand, contains 128 pieces, of which 101 are proofs in the first state (see also Bartsch, p. 234). Two of them belong to the lost blocks, which are not found in the edition of 1796, and which have not been described by Bartsch, viz. :—

1. Jerome of Heremberg, as Chief of a Column, and holding the Tablet with Verses, is seen on horseback heading the train.

This piece belongs to those which are found under the Nos. 125 to 129, which have been erroneously numbered in the edition of 1796, as follows :—

No. 125,† erroneously numbered 128.
No. 126,   „   „   129.
No. 127,   „   „   125.
No. 128,   „   „   127.
No. 129,   „   „   126.
No. 129*, J. de Heremberg, wanting.

2. The Triumphal Car, with Philip I. and Joanna of Castile, who holds the Arms of Castile and Arragon.

This piece ought to follow No. 135, where a genius drives a team of four horses. The water-mark of these two leaves is an escutcheon, with a sickle in the centre.†

† See the editor's notice of the plates of the "Triumph."

Passavant's Additions to Bartsch's List of Wood Engravings.

83. Carrying the Cross. The two thieves head the procession. At the right, on the first plane, St. Veronica holds the sudarium ; on the left, a child, who carries some nails and a vessel with vinegar. A crowd of people follow. At the bottom is written, " O Herr Jesu Christe ich ermane dich des gangs und ausfürens do du dz schwar creutz," &c., and the date, 1527.

Eight leaves joined, treated in exactly the same manner, and of the same dimensions, as " Christ on the Mount of Olives " (Bartsch, No. 17, vol. vii. p. 205) and " Christ on the Cross " (Bartsch, No. 19). *h.* 32$\frac{9}{13}$ inches, *w.* 24 inches.* Albertine collection at Vienna.

84. The Virgin, half-length. She is standing, and holds the Infant Jesus, who caresses her ; towards the left, and with both hands before her. In her right hand she holds a crown of roses. The arch which is above her is adorned with rosettes.

We find proofs of this piece in black, and others in chiaroscuro, but in which the darkest tints are put in with the brush. *h.* 10$\frac{10}{12}$ inches, *w.* 5$\frac{7}{13}$ inches. Berlin.

85. St. Anne. She is seated beside the Virgin, standing at her left, who presents to her the Infant Jesus. Below, at the foot, the signature H B. *h.* 4$\frac{8}{13}$ inches, *w.* 3$\frac{4}{13}$ inches. Munich.

86. St. Helena, St. Bridget, and St. Elizabeth. These three standing figures are marked H B, then " Jost de Negker zu Augspurg." Paris.

87—98. Twelve Leaves of the Apocalypse.

They are all marked with the initials H B, but are too weak to be the work of the older Burgmair. The compositions are often borrowed from Durer, and therefore must be by the younger Burgmair. *h.* 6 inches, *w.* 4$\frac{10}{12}$ inches. They first appeared in

---

* Passavant is in error, as in Bartsch Nos. 17 and 19 differ in size. No. 19 is thus given : height 32 inches, margin at base 3 inches, width 24 inches.

the New Testament printed by Sylvain Ottmar, at Augsburg, in 1523. Folio.

(87.) Christ standing in the clouds, his eyes shooting flames, &c. Mark at the right.

(88.) God enthroned, surrounded with emblems of the four Evangelists, &c. Mark at bottom, at right.

(89.) The Distribution of Trumpets to the Angels, &c.

(90.) St. John eating the book.

(91.) Two men standing before the dragon, &c.

(92.) The Angels pour out vials of wrath, &c.

(93.) The Scarlet woman, &c.

(94.) The horseman called faithful and true, &c.

(95.) The Angel casting the millstone, &c.

(96.) The woman standing on the crescent and the dragon with seven heads, &c.

(97.) The Angel binding the dragon with the chain. Marked at bottom, at left.

(98.) The Angel shows to St. John the new Jerusalem, &c. Marked in middle, at bottom.

99. The Emperor Maximilian hearing High Mass. (Bartsch, vol. vii. p. 184, No. 31.) *h.* $10\frac{7}{12}$ inches, *w.* $7\frac{4}{12}$ inches. The Emperor is kneeling before a priedieu in the background, on the right; more in front the choristers, and opposite to them the organist. In the extreme distance is the celebrant, accompanied by his deacons. Above are suspended the Imperial arms, with the double and the single eagle, as well as those of the Medici with the seven pales,* perhaps those of the Pope Leo X.

Ancient proofs bear the following inscription in three lines :— " Imperator Caesar Divus Maximilianus pius foelix Augustus Christianitatis supremus Princeps Germanie, &c., transiit Anno Christi Domini MDXIX. Die XII. mensis Januarii, regni Romani XXXIII. Hungariæ vero XXIX. Vixit Anno LIX. Mensibus IX. Diebus XIX."

Another impression has above the inscription, " Ein hüpsch spruch von Kaiser Maximilian ;" and below a German inscription

* The arms of the Medici were six pellets. —ED.

in eighteen verses, and below the verses, "Antony Formschneider zu Frankfordt."

This fine wood-engraving resembles so much the drawing of Hans Burgmair, particularly in the illustrations to Petrarks Trost-spiegel, that there is no doubt that it ought to be attributed to him. The cutting, which much resembles that of Lützelburger, is done by an excellent wood-engraver, of whom we have no notice except that furnished by the above signature.

100. Piece commemorative of the Emperor Maximilian I.

The three wood-engravings which are found have each an ex-planatory inscription, and on each side, in six columns, a relation in Latin of the last events of the life of the Emperor, and of his death, happening on the 12th of January, 1519, at Wels, in Austria; also concerning the funeral pomp which ensued : the whole by Dr. James Mennel, Chancellor of the Order of St. John, and historiographer to the Emperor. *h.* 18 inches, *w.* 14 inches. Imperial Library at Vienna. See F. v. Bartsch, No. 2569.

    a. Christ on the Cross, between the Virgin and St. John. The medallion is surrounded by a broad ribbon, with twelve shields of the military religious orders. The wood of the Cross, with the head and arms of the Saviour, as well as the shield of the Imperial arms, "contre-coticé d'argent," and surrounded,with the collar of the Order of the Golden Fleece, outreach above and below the above-mentioned ribbon. Diameter 9$\frac{9}{13}$ inches.

The inscription is as follows :—

"De divi Maximiliani Romanorum Cesaris Christiana vita Et felicissimo eius obitu, &c., ad reverendissimũ in Christo patrem et illustrem principem Fabriciũ da Carreto ex marchionibus finalis sacrosancte domus Hospitalis sancti Joannis Jherosolimitani Mili-taris ordinis Magnum magistrum Rhodi rc. ut precipuũ Cesaris obsequentẽ Jacobi Manlij doctoris, eiusdem ordinis in Germania Cancellarii r dicti Cesaris hystoriographi Hystoria. De his quibus potissime iam corpore egrotante animum reficiebat Cesar."

    b. The Monarch weakened by Sickness. He is seated on a throne placed near his bed, and listens with attention, surrounded by five courtiers, to the genealogist Manlius (Mennel), who reads from a folio volume by the light of a candle. *h.* 4 inches, *w.* 6 inches.

The inscription is as follows :—

" Cesari antiquissime et nobilissime Genealogie eius per Manlium libri leguntur."

    c. The Coffin of the Emperor. It is covered with a mortuary cloth embroidered with gold, and surmounted with a Crucifix between four chandeliers or candelabra. Some canons, seated in two rows, sing the Service of the Dead from the books of the Choir. *h.* $3\frac{8}{13}$ inches, *w.* $11\frac{3}{13}$ inches.

Inscription :—

" De felicissimo Cesaris obitu, et exanimi corpore sub crucifixi et militaribus S. Georgii insignibus ad sarcophagum deposito."

101. The Emperor Charles V. and the Hermit. The Emperor, yet Prince of Burgundy, in hunting costume, speaks with a hermit at the entrance of a wood. The latter is standing at the right. The mark is below, at the left. *h.* $5\frac{4}{13}$ inches, *w.* $3\frac{4}{13}$ inches.

102. The Emperor Charles V. between Vice and Virtue. He is clad in a travelling dress between the two allegorical figures, Virtus et Voluptas. This last is on the right, at the entrance to a wood. The mark is below, at the right. *h.* $5\frac{4}{13}$ inches, *w.* $3\frac{4}{12}$ inches.

    These two wood-engravings are found in a book entitled : "Contenta hoc libello. Virtus et Voluptas, Carmen de origine ducum Austrie. Aegloga : Coridon et Philetus rustici. Ad lectorem est gratus parvis noñunqm̃ fructus in hortis, quod placeat parvus sepe libellus habet." In fine : Distichon. "Invidia nostra periit pars maxima fame. Invidia nostrum scandet ad astra decus. Salutem ex inimicis nostris V. G. M. Magister Johannes Othmar calcographus formis excusit. Auguste apud edem dive Ursule cis Lychū. Anno M.D.XII. XXXI Julii." In 4to. See R. Weigel's Cat., No. 21115.

103. Four Leaves, each containing a king, standing.

    These are clad in a fantastic manner, like the bronze statues at the tomb of Maximilian I. at Insbruck. Folio, each signed with the initials H B. They were found in a stitched book containing besides fifty-three etchings of the younger Burgmair, representing knights in armour, and which is preserved in the collection of the Stutgard Museum.

104. Chronicle of the Family of the Counts Truchsess of Waldburg, written by Matthew von Bappenhaim. (Die Fa-
milien-Chronik des Grafen Truchsesen von Waldburg
geschrieben von Matheus von Bappenhaim `d. heil.
Röm. Reichs Erbmarschalckh, beider Rechten Doctor
und Thumherr zu Augspurg.)

This is the title of a manuscript, in folio, on parchment, containing the figures engraved on wood of 71 members of this family,
and of which 68 were designed in 1530 by Hans Burgmair. The
69th is signed C A; the two following have no mark, and are not
by Burgmair; the 72nd, with the signature Herr Jacob T. geb,
1512, is a coloured drawing. This interesting book belongs to
the rich collection of engravings of the Prince of Wolfegg, in
his château of the same name near to Ravensburg, where there
is also another copy on paper, with the engravings coloured, as in
the preceding.

The first engraving shows us the author, Matthew de Bappen-
heim, seated at a round table, covered with books and writing.
Signed 1530, H B.

The second represents " Herrn Gebhardt der Erst," whose arms
are three fir-cones, the shield surmounted with a helmet crowned,
crested with a fir-tree; arms which are again found in the following pieces, except those at the last, where the shield bears
three lions.* We see on some of them the arms of Sonnenberg,
a mount with four summits, crowned with rays. The figures are
standing, some of them in fantastic armour, on a white ground.
Fifty leaves bear the signature below, H B; the others are not
signed, but they have been designed by our artist. Nagler, in
his Dictionary, mentions another copy of this rare work as existing in the collection at Munich.

105. The book entitled " Schimpff vnnd Ernst " (Dass Buch
Schimpff vnnd Ernst—von Joh. Pauli—gedruckt zu
Augspurg durch Heinrich Stainer). Folio.

The most ancient edition is, as it appears, without date. New
editions of the book were published by the same editor in the
years 1526, 1534, 1535, 1536, 1537, 1542, 1544, 1546. The first

* The Truchsess sprung originally from Tann, in Swabia, and hence the
three fir-cones (Tannenzapfen) in their arms. One of them became, under
Conradin (of the dynasty of Hohenstaufen), minister of this monarch in
Germany, and received from him the arms with the three lions.

six editions contain 40 engravings on wood, of which 33 are by
Hans Burgmair, two by Schaeuflein (Bartsch, Nos. 85, 86 ; vol. vii.
p. 264), and the five others by a mediocre artist of the Augsburg school.   The three last editions have only 35 engravings.
h. 5 $\frac{5}{13}$ or $\frac{8}{12}$ inches, *w.* 5 $\frac{9}{13}$ or $\frac{10}{12}$ inches ; or, *h.* 3 $\frac{7}{13}$ or $\frac{8}{13}$ inches,
w. 5 $\frac{9}{13}$ inches.

106. Petrarch, the Book of Fortune.   ("Petrarca's Glückbuch,
    Beydes dess Guten und Bösen ;" or thus, "Trostspiegel
    in Glück und Ungluck," etc.)   The most ancient edition
    known has this title : "Franciscus Petrarcha.   Von des
    Artzney bayder Glück, des guten und widerwertigen.   Und
    wess sich ein yeder inn gelück und unglück halten sol.
    Auss dem lateinischen in das Teutsch gezogen.   Mit
    kunstlichen figuren durchauss gantz lustig und schön
    gezyeret. 2 Theile. Augspurg. H. Stainer, 1532." Folio,
    with 259 wood-engravings.

Stainer says in his preface that the engravings have been made
"after the figured compositions [visierlicher Angebung] of Dr.
Sebastian Brandt," by which he wishes to say that the invention
of the subjects belongs partly to the latter, whilst the drawings of
these compositions for the wood-engraver have been made by our
master.

Other editions of Stainer appeared at Augsburg in 1539 and
1545, and were followed by those of Egenolf, at Frankfort-on-the
Maine, in 1551, 1559, 1572, and 1584 ; and in the same city by
those of John Saur, under the firm of Vinc Steinmeyer, in 1604
and 1620.   All these editions are in folio.

The numerous engravings which are found (they mount up to
260 in the Frankfort editions) appear in part in the book of
"Schimpff und Ernst" and in the Cicero.   They appear nearly
all to belong to the older Burgmair, though they do not bear his
signature.   Some of them have a mark like an S recumbent, ∾
which appears to indicate a wood-engraver.

On the first leaf the author, Francis Petrarch, is in a room
writing his book ; on the second, which is accompanied by a
piece of poetry by Sebastian Brandt, the author holds a balance
with vessels in which he pours water.   On the verso of this leaf
is represented a wheel of fortune, with four figures of kings.   In
some editions we see a second wheel of fortune, where the king,
who is seated above, does not bear a sceptre.   On one little

wheel turned by Fortune herself, with her eyes bandaged, a crowned ass is seen at the top of the wheel. The last leaf contains an allegorical representation of the useless care which the dying take about their interment. It bears the date 1520.

107. The Offices of Cicero. (Officia M. T. C. Ein buch so Marcus Tullius Cicero der Römer, zu seynem Sune Marco. Von den tugendsamen ämptern, &c. Gedrückt in der keyserlichen Statt Augspurg durch Heinrichen Stayner. Vollendet am XVI. Tag Februarij Im M.DXXXI. Jar.) Folio.

It is the first edition of the book of John of Schwarzenberg, with 104 wood-engravings, mostly of octavo size, but of which, the only piece, marked H B, is that described by Bartsch (No. 74), "Six Doctors seated round a table." All of the others bear notwithstanding so decidedly the imprint of the style of Hans Burgmair, that we cannot hesitate to attribute them to him. We ought to remark that in the composition forming the division to the third book, entitled, "Was in gemeinen Kaufhändeln der Ehren und Nutzbarkeytnach, sich geziemen möge," we see on the

counter of a ship the letters H bb. and on the gate of the

city H W of which the first belong perhaps to Burgmair the younger, whilst the last indicate the engraver. The large engraving before the title-page represents Cicero, who gives his book to a messenger, who is to deliver it to his son; and the last à buffoon, who, laughing, crowns a sow.

The second and third editions of this book were issued by the same bookseller in 1531, April 29 and December 7. Successive editions appeared at Augsburg, August 3, 1532, October 1, 1533, November 13, 1535, November 27, 1537, December 13, 1540, and lastly, November 3, 1545.

Christian Egenolf, of Frankfort-on-the-Maine, afterwards obtained the blocks, and brought out the following editions :—

"Vonn Gebüre und billigkeit. Des Fürtrefflichen, hochberümpten Römers Marci Tullij Ciceronis, drei Bücher an seinen Sohn Marcum, Von Gebürlichen Werken, &c. Gedruckt zu Franckfurt an Mayn bei Christian Egenolff, M.D.L. Im Jenner." Folio.

" Officia Ciceronis das ist vonn Gebürlichen Werken, Wolstand vnnd Rechtthun, etc. Gedruckt zu Franckfurt am Mayn bey Christian Egenolffs Erben. MDLXV. Im Jenner."

As the works of Schwarzenberg were very curious, Henry Stainer, of Augsburg, collected and printed them in a single volume, of which he produced several editions, which all bear the following title, beginning with Cicero :—

"Der Teutsch Cicero. Warumb das buch also genent, auch inhalts solches beyde erkleert, so dieses blatt wird umgewendt. M.D.XXXIII."

"Der Teutsch Cicero, etc. Vollendet am 8 Marz 1535."

"Der Teutsch Cicero, etc. Wider fleyssig ersehen vnd gedruckt. Anno MDXXXX." Folio.

According to Ebert, "Dictionnaire Bibliographique," there was an edition in 8vo., published in 1562 by Köpfel, at Worms.

The illustrations of the Cicero were in part used for the book entitled—

"Fürnemste Historien und exempel von widerwertigen Glück, etc. durch etc. Joannem Boccatium, etc. Augspurg, H. Stainer, 1545." Folio.

108. The Lives of Sts. Ulric, Symprecht, and Afra. (Das leben, verdienen und wunderwerk der heiligen Augspurgs bistumbs bischoffen, Sant Ulrichs und Symprecht auch der säligen martrerin Sant Aphre, irer muter Hilarie geschlecht und gesellschaft, in unserem daselbst loblichen gotshauss verstand. Augspurg, gedruckt durch Silvanum Ottmar, 1516.)

This book contains six wood-engravings :—

    a. The border of the Title. At the sides, two columns; above, an arabesque with two angels. *h.* 6 inches, *w.* $4\frac{6}{15}$ inches, as in the four following pieces.

    b. Sts. Ulric, Symprecht, and Afra. Full length, standing under a porch. Below, three shields.

    c. St. Ulric. Full length, with the border of the title.

    d. St. Symprecht. Full length, with the same border.

    e. St. Afra. Full length, ditto.

    f. A Church, with the inscription, "Ain form visier und vorreissung der angefangen Kirchen Sant Ulrichs und Aphren zu Augspurg." *h.* $6\frac{6}{11}$ inches, *w.* 5 inches. It is the last leaf of the book.

See R. Weigel, Catalogue No. 16353, but he does not say if the pieces bear the signature of the master.

109. The Battle of St. Ulric.   The Emperor is accompanied to the field by the Saint-Bishop, to whom an angel brings a cross.   At the left, below, on a shield, is the date, 1520.

This piece has been described wrongly by Bartsch in the works of Lucas Cranach (No. 74), though it belongs decidedly to Burgmair.   *h.* 6$\frac{8}{12}$ inches, *w.* 4$\frac{9}{12}$ inches.

110. The Steersman.   On a large ship is seen at the helm a man of condition, clad like a savant, and who raises his left hand to speak.   At the right, below, are the initials H B. *h.* 6$\frac{8}{12}$ inches, *w.* 4$\frac{1}{12}$ inches.

On the back of this piece, in the impression in the Munich Cabinet, we find Latin verses with these words : "Venerabili Viro dño Georgio Reysch : patri ac priori, etc. friburgo A. 1510," which may enable us to trace the book in which it is to be found.

111. The Changes of Fortune.   This piece is divided into six compartments, three and three in two rows.   They are separated from each other by columns, and each contains two figures, representing a rich and a poor man in conversation.   Above we read, on a bandrol "Wie der Arm rich wirt vnd der Reich arm."

See Brulliot, "Table générale des Monogrammes," &c., p. 491.

112. A Child with Three Legs.   This monstrosity is represented twice : at the left, seated on a cushion, and *vis-à-vis*, lying down.   Below, at the right, the signature H B.   Above, this inscription, "Disz Künd ist geboren worden zu Tettnang."   Below, an explanatory text.   *h.* 3$\frac{1}{12}$ inches, *w.* 5$\frac{9}{12}$ inches, without the inscriptions.

Noticed by Brulliot, "Table," &c., who had seen a copy which bore, above, a shield with the date 1516.

113. The Column with the Vase emitting flames.   On a column at the right a vase is seen, from whence flames issue. Three peasants are on their knees in adoration ; some others appear to run off to rejoin a large troop with cattle that are seen in the distance.   At the left, below, the initials H B.   *h.* 2$\frac{6}{12}$ inches, *w.* 3$\frac{1}{4}$$\frac{9}{4}$ inches.   (Albertine Collection at Vienna.)

114. A Manual (Täschenbüchlin).

> " Aus einem closter in dem Riess
> Kompt dieses Täschenbüchlin süss
> Das der Mensch sol bey jm tragen
> Und damit sein veind verjagen."

Augspurg, Hans Miller, 1516. 8vo.

Of the fourteen engravings which adorn this little book, ten belong to Hans Burgmair, one is used twice (the four others are by Hans Schaufelein). *h.* 3¼⅔ inches, *w.* 2⁹⁄₁₃ inches.

a. God the Father giving his benediction.
b. The Annunciation.
c. The Sacrifice of the Mass.
d. Christ on the Cross, between the Virgin and St. John. This piece repeated as the tenth engraving.
e. The Mass of St. Gregory.
f. St. George killing the dragon.
g. Sts. Sebastian and St. Roch.
h. The Last Supper.
i. The Prayer of St. Thomas Aquinas to God the Father. With the signature of the master.

(See R. Weigel, Catalogue, No. 18771.)

115. A Chronicle. (Eine schöne Chronik uñ Hystoria, wye nach der Synndtflut Noe, die Teutschen, das streitbar volck jren anfang empfangen haben, besonder den ersten namen Schwaben gehaissen worden, Wa und wie sy vō ersten gewont. . . . Auch dar bey von der Kayserlichen Statt Augspurg, etc. (published by Meisterlen). Augspurg, Melchior Ramminger, 1522. fol.) The title, with St. Ulric and St. Afra, bears the initials of Burgmair.

Amongst other wood-engravings there is a copy, after Schauflein, of the battle of St. Ulric by the master HS (see Brulliot, Dict., i. No. 2502). This monogram is attributed to the printer, Henry Steiner of Augsburg, who was probably also a wood-engraver. (See Weigel, Kunstcat. No. 18772.)

116. The Banquet. (Ein nutzlich Regiment der gesundtheyt genant das Vanquete oder gastmal der Edlen Diener von der Complexion, etc. gemacht durch . . . Dr. Hein. Ludovicum de Avila . . . durch Mich. Krautwadel verteutscht, etc. Augsburg, H. Steyner, 1531. 4to.)

In this book of medicine we find six wood-engravings of middling quality, of which one, the portrait of the doctor Avila, bears the signature of H. Burgmair. The Spanish edition, " Vanquete de nobles cavalleros, etc. Vindelicorum Urbe Augusta —per industriosum virum Henr. Stainer chalcotypū." S. A. 4to. contains eight more engravings, in all 14 pieces, which are all attributed to our master. (See R. Weigel, Cat. Nos. 12857 and 19438, and Wiechmann-Kadow, in Naumann's "Archives," ii. p. 158.)

117. The Brotherhood of Fools (Schelmenzunft-durch . . . Thoman Murner von Strassburg. Augsburg, S. Otmar, 1513 et 1514. 4to.)

The first of the 40 engravings in the book represents the author with the inscription, "DOCTOR LAVX," and bears the initials H B. The others are equally attributed to Hans Burgmair, but appear to be inferior work. (See Wiechmann-Kadow, in Naumann's "Archives," ii. p. 158.)

118. Portrait of Conrad Celtes. Half-length, turned slightly to the left, under an arch richly adorned, on which is written the inscription, "EXITVS. ACTA PROBAT. QVI BENE FECIT HABET." He rests his hands on four volumes of his works, which bear upon the edges the following titles : "GER. ILLVS.—AMOR. EPIGRA.—ODAR." At the sides below are seated two little genii weeping, and in the corners above are Apollo and Mercury. The arms of Celtes, a shield broken in the middle, are seen at the lower margin, with an inscription beginning :

"D. M. S.

FLETE PII VATES ET TVNDITE PECTORA PALMIS"
and ending—
"HIC IN CHRIS. QVIESCIT VIXIT AN. IXL. SAL
SESQVIMILL ET VII.
SVB DIVO MAXIMIL. AVGVST."

Before him, the broken shield of his arms bears two C's adorsed, and two pallets, accompanied by three stars. On the margin, below, H B.

This piece, so far from having been engraved in honour of the poet after his death, was done for Celtes himself during his lifetime, and he presented it to his friends. As he died the following year, they changed the false date 1507 to "MDVIII Mensis Februarij, Die IV." (See Naumann's "Archives," 1856, ii. p. 143.)

119. Portrait of James Fugger. A bust in profile, turned to the left, and the head dressed with a band. Inscription, "Jacobus Fugger Civis Augustus."

This piece, engraved by Jost de Necker in a very delicate and graceful manner, is an impression in colour—red, brown, and black. The drapery in green, on a white ground, gives a charming effect. $h.$ 8$\frac{8}{13}$ inches, $w.$ 6 inches. (Butsch collection at Augsburg. Berlin.)

120. The great Imperial Eagle. It is printed in black, and contains several allegorical subjects. On the neck is seated the Emperor, and beside him, two heralds of arms. Below flows a stream, with the inscription, "FONS MVSARVM," and close to it the initials H B. In the basin are seated the nine muses, below them the seven liberal arts, and still lower, a composition represents Paris roused by Mercury to deliver his judgment on the beauty of the three goddesses standing before him; at the right, Discord, kneeling, presents to him the golden apple. Near we read, "MERCVR—DISCORDIA." On the feathers of the wings are fourteen medallions, in two series of seven, containing the days of the Creation and the seven liberal arts. Above, the inscription:—

"LAVREA SERTA GERIT SACRO JOVIS ALESINORE, MAXIMILIANIS JAM CELEBRATA SCOLIS;"

And further off—

"AQVILA DIVVS IMPERIALIS DIVINA FABRICA MAXIMI H. VANA INVETA."

Below :—

"BVRGKMAIR HANC AQVILAM DEPINXERAT ARTE
JOHÁES ET CELTIS PVLCHRAM TEXVIT HIS-
TORIAM.—ILLE NOVEM MVSIS SEPTENAS JVNX-
ERAT ARTES QVAS STVDIO PARILI DOCTA
VIENA COLIT."

h. 12$\frac{8}{13}$ inches, *w.* 8$\frac{6}{13}$ inches. (Albertine collection at Vienna,
Basle, Munich.)

121. The Imperial Eagle. On a shield is the Imperial eagle,
crowned, bearing on its breast the shield of Austria. The
helmet is crested by a vol. Inscription: "ARMA ET
INSIGNIA SACR. ROM. IMPERII. 1515."
Below, at the sides of the shield, the letters H—B.
h. 7$\frac{8}{13}$ inches, *w.* 6 inches. Basle.

122. The Single Eagle. The eagle is printed in black on a
white ground, bearing on its breast the arms of Austria;
party per fess. Marked below, H B. *h.* 7$\frac{4}{13}$ inches,
w. 5$\frac{1}{4}$ inches. Berlin.

123. The Arms with the two Crescents. Party per pale with the
two crescents facing. Surmounted by an open helmet
crested by a demi-figure of the Virgin holding in each
hand a crescent. At right, at bottom, the mark H B
small. *h.* 5 inches, *w.* 4 inches. Basle.

124. The Arms with the crest of the winged Lion. Per saltier,
argent, and sable charged with a lion, argent. The
closed helmet is crested by a demi-lion, winged. At
right, at bottom, the mark H B very small. *h.* 6$\frac{1}{4}$ inches,
w. 4$\frac{3}{4}$ inches. Basle.

125. The Arms with the Griffin rampant. Quarterly, argent
and sable. Four griffins counter-changed. Over all, an
escutcheon party per fess, in chief a demi-lion, in base
a chevron *pignonné*. The helmet is surmounted by a
crown between the plumes of a peacock. Not marked.
h. 7$\frac{1}{4}$ inches, *w.* 4$\frac{1}{4}$ inches. Basle.

126. The Arms with the two Lions argent. Quarterly, first and
fourth sable; a lion, argent; second and third fretty,
argent, and sable. The helmet is crested with a lion,
sejant, crowned, between two demi-vols. Basle.

127. The Arms with an Eagle debruised by a saltier. The eagle sable. The shield is surmounted by a crowned helmet, which is crested by a demi-eagle, crowned; charged with St. Andrew's cross, argent. Basle.

128. The Shield with the head of Æolus. It is turned to the dexter, and the helmet is crested by the representation of a field. The escutcheon is on a black background, and surmounted by an arch having at the springs two angels' heads. *h.* 8¾ inches, *w.* 5⁸⁄₁₃ inches. Basle.

129. The Arms with the Lilies. Argent; a cinquefoil, gules : impaling, gules ; lilies couped, argent. The helmet is crested with lilies between two demi-vols. Marked H B at right. *h.* 14 inches, *w.* 9 inches (?). (Albertine Collection at Vienna.)

130. Initials, with Children. 1521. There are 23 initials in the roman character, with the children, who are playing. They are detached in white on a black ground. They are enclosed in a square with two lines of border. The 24th compartment, a circle inside a square, concludes the series. Below is printed : " Gedruckt zu Augspurg durch Jost De Necker," or only " Jost de Negker zu Augspurg," and near the last letter the date 1521.

In neither of the two editions is the signature of Burgmair, but in the impression at Basle his name is in writing ; besides, the design and style of the children and of the ornaments are absolutely in the manner of the master ; and the belief that it is his work receives again more force from the circumstance that it was engraved by Jost de Necker at Augsburg.

The third edition of the Initials bears likewise, near the letter Z, the date 1521 ; but we find on a ball near the letter F the monogram, slightly crooked, of Albert Durer, which has given recently ground for the opinion that it was designed by this master. A mutilated impression, containing 22 initials, belonging formerly to an amateur at Nuremberg, came into the possession of Mr. R. Weigel at Leipsic (see Kunstcat. No. 19099), who had executed for his work, entitled " Holzschnitte berühmter Meister," two facsimiles of the letters A and F.

These initials, cut on two blocks, were not destined for the ornamentation of books, but rather to serve as models, as is

abundantly proved by the fact that the tail of the letter Q en-
croaches on the ground of the letter R, and indeed they are not
found in any of the Augsburg editions.

We find, however, ancient copies in many publications at Basle,
Cologne, and Nuremburg; amongst others, in the book which
bears the title :—

"Theophylacti Enarrationes in quatuor Evangel. Basileæ,
Cratander, 1525."

And in :—

"Ex recognitione Des. Erasmi Roterodami. C. Suetonius
Tranquillus. Dion. Cassius. Nicæus. Aelius Spartanus etc.
Coloniæ in aedibus Euch. Cervicorni. 1527."

And probably in the anatomical work of Volcker Coiter, Nuremberg 1572 and 1575, folio. All these copies exhibit striking
differences. The better reproductions do not exhibit the letters
in white on a black ground, but are divided into two parts by a
line, and have one side shaded. The compartments have three
lines of border. Some have a thin line at the left of the initials.
The third copy has the letters in white, but the cutting is so
bad that it is immediately seen to be a counterfeit.

The first edition of the alphabet, as well as the second,
is always printed on two folio leaves, $10\frac{4}{12}$ inches high and
$5\frac{4}{12}$ inches wide, and each letter is from 2 inches to $2\frac{1}{12}$ inches
square.

The subjects are as follows :—

A. Two children are blowing horns; that at the left presents
its back. Above, a shell.

B. Six children, in part furnished with wings. One of them
plays the bagpipes; another, at the right, the dulcimer.
Above, a fabulous bird.

C. Three children; the middle one is winged and riding on a
roebuck.

D. Three children; the middle one rides on a dolphin and
holds a standard.

E. Two children sitting amongst reeds. One of them holds
a crane fastened by a string. Below, at the right, a
monkey.

F. Four little Cupids playing. That seated at the right rests
on a ball, which, in the last edition, bears the monogram
of Durer, crooked, which is never so found in his works.

P

G. Four children. One at the right pours a liquid from a flagon into a basin, in which another child is seated.

H. Three children. One in the middle is seated and playing on a double pipe.

I. Four children. One is seated in a basket, and drawn by one of his companions on all-fours.

K. Three children at the left, and a bear dancing at the right.

L. Five children. One of them rides on a stick carried by the others.

M. Four winged children. One of them is standing on the backs of two others lying on the ground.

N. Five children, some winged. The second, to the right, holds a flytrap above another kneeling in front.

O. Six children, some winged. In the midst of them a buffoon.

P. Six children, mostly winged, play together. Two among them rest their hands on the ground.

Q. Four children carry another in triumph, after the manner of Bacchus. At the left, and in the middle, two other children are partly visible.

R. Three children play at cards. Above is seen a fourth with his back turned.

S. Three children going hunting with a dog and a falcon. They go towards the left.

T. Two children ride on seahorses.

V. Five children, two of whom hold a string.

X. Five winged children, two playing music.

Y. Five children play at soldiers. They march towards the right. Two of them ride wooden horses.

Z. Two children are standing near an urn, and hold labels with the date 1521.*

---

* Other initials are seen with the children playing; amongst others, the figures which are used in the books printed by Steyner of Augsburg, and which may be attributed with great probability to Hans Burgmair. Weichmann-Kadow has described several in Naumann's "Archives," i. p. 126; and we refer to what he has said in the hope that further researches will lead to a satisfactory result on this point.

ETCHINGS BY BURGMAIR THE YOUNGER.

1. Venus and Mars. *h.* 6$\frac{8}{12}$ inches, *w.* 4$\frac{3}{4}$ inches. (Bartsch, vii. p. 199, No. 1.)

The bookseller Stöckel of Vienna had, in 1820, the original plate, from which he took some impressions.

2. The Arms of the town of Augsburg. The shield, with the fir-cone on the capital of a column, has as supporters two griffins. Below, in two bandrols, "HE VOGTHERR, H. BVRGKMAI," and above, 1545. *h.* 7$\frac{3}{4}$ inches, *w.* 5$\frac{1}{12}$ inches.

The handling is exactly the same as No. 1, and, judging by the date, this is the work of the younger Burgmair. These arms are found in the book mentioned below, No. 3, which does not, however, seem to have appeared till 1618.

3. The Escutcheons, with supporters, of noble families of Augsburg. 80 leaves. *h.* 7$\frac{3}{4}$ inches, *w.* 5$\frac{1}{4}$ inches.

The supporters are, for the most part, figures, covered with fanciful heraldic ornaments, resembling the statues on the sepulchral monument of Maximilian I. at Innspruck. Beside each is the shield. None of these leaves bear a mark, and in the first editions the names of the families even are wanting. The first edition probably appeared about 1545, since the Arms of Augsburg, mentioned above, serve as the title-page and bear that date. These arms have the names of H. Burgmair and Henry Vogtherr, who appear to have been associated in the execution of these etchings. According to Nagler, this first edition only contained twenty-three plates, and is entitled "Arms and Supporters of some noble Families of the town of the Holy Roman Empire Augsburg."—"Wappen und derselben Wappenhaltern einiger Adelichen Geschlechte in der heil. Rom. Reichsstadt Augsbourg."

In the collection of prints at Stuttgard there is a book containing fifty-three proofs of these etchings in the first state, partly numbered, and one of which bears the number 50, as well as some original pen-and-ink drawings by Burgmair and by other hands, dated 1547. It may be inferred that there was then in contemplation a more extended edition than that with twenty-three plates, and that such an edition may have appeared about 1547.

The edition in folio, largely supplemented by Zimmermann, and containing 80 plates, appeared at Augsburg in 1618, under the following title :

"Ernewrtes Geschlechterbuch der löblichen desz heiligen Reichs Statt Augspurg Patriciorum darunder 80 vorausz lustige zierliche contrafacturen, der Schild, Helm und Wappen Ehregemeldter Geschlechtern von weylandt der Kunstreichern Mahlern in Augspurg, Johann Burckmair und Heinrichen Vogtherr von Anno 1545 in Stahel zierlich geradiert, die übrigen von Wilhelm Peter Zimmerman auffs fleissigst hinzugethan worden, &c. 1618."

On the title-page are the Arms of Augsburg, already mentioned, with the date, 1545.

The entire work is divisible into three parts. In the first should be placed the pages 1, 3, 6, 7, 10, 13, 16, 19, 22, 23, 25, 26, 27, 28, 31, 32, 37, 39, 46, 47, 49, which are boldly executed in the style of Burgmair. Others, similar in style, but executed with a finer point, are without any doubt by Henry Vogtherr. The remainder are very inferior, and form the portion added by Zimmermann.

4. The Virgin and Infant Jesus. She is standing in a landscape, and supports with her right arm the infant Jesus, who passes his arms round her neck. She carries a palm in the left hand, and her long hair floats towards the right. On the same side is a slender tree, and another, thicker. At the right a rocky landscape. _h._ 6 inches, _w._ 4 inches. Berlin.

This etching, without signature, is indeed treated entirely in the manner of Burgmair, but it has at the same time very considerable analogy to another etching, in the style of Burgmair, executed by the master Jaccop, described No. 1, under the heading "Le Maître Jaccop" (vol. iii. p. 287), and might well be his work.

TRIUMPH

OF THE EMPEROR

MAXIMILIAN

In a succession of a hundred and thirty-five
wood engravings after the
designs
of

HANS BURGMAIR.

With the Ancient Description dictated by the
Emperor to his secretary Marc Treitzsaurwein.

Printed at Vienna by Matthias André Schmidt, printer
to the Court, and sold in London,
by J. Edwards, Pall Mall.

PREFACE.

(*Translated from the Edition of* 1796.)

———0———

AMONGST the works relating to literature and the arts, which were the fruits of the leisure of the Emperor Maximilian I., his Triumph deserves to be placed in the first rank. Destined, like the Theurdanck and the Weiss Kunig, to serve as a monument of his grandeur, the Emperor there represents the circumstances of his house, his pleasures, his territorial possessions, his wars, his conquests, and many other events in his reign, by a procession of several hundred figures, of which some on foot, others on horseback, or drawn in cars, form a very magnificent triumphal cortége.

This Triumph was at first executed in miniature of the most precious work, on a hundred and nine sheets of parchment, of the extraordinary size of thirty-four inches in length, and twenty inches in height; forming a work, which, for its magnitude, and the richness of its execution, deserves to be placed amongst the most precious works of this kind. It is now in the Imperial Library,* amongst the most important manuscripts it possesses.

The Emperor, probably not wishing to confine the pleasure of a work so important, to himself, or rather desiring to render it a lasting monument by multiplying it, had it engraved on wood; and it is the collection of these engravings which is now offered to the public.

It consists of a hundred and thirty-five pieces, precious

* Vienna.

specimens of the art of wood-engraving, which for their spirit and beauty of design, as well as for the care and skill of their cutting, deserve the attention and approbation of all connoisseurs. Sandrart, an acknowledged authority, and who had seen a part of these engravings, characterizes them as the finest that have ever been produced. Many other connoisseurs have arrived at nearly the same conclusion. But may-be not to the artist alone will they be interesting, as, offering exact designs of costume, armour, instruments, manners and customs of the time of Maximilian, they may prove useful to the historian in search of facts and evidence.

On this account, it is to be regretted that this work is a fragment. Forty blocks were preserved in the cabinet of curiosities at Ambras, in the Tyrol, where in all probability they had remained from the death of the Emperor; the other ninety-five were found at the Jesuits' College at Gratz, in Styria, without any information as to how they got there, until they were both transmitted to Vienna in 1779, and deposited in the Imperial Library.

Following the drawings painted in miniature, where each leaf contains the subject of two of the wood-engravings, the number of the latter ought to reach above two hundred if the work had been carried to a conclusion. The two sets of blocks having been found in two different places, there was room for conjecture that a third, concealed from our observation, might lie hidden in some other cabinet or library. Following out this idea, the most industrious search was made; but it was altogether fruitless; and as up to this day nothing has been discovered, we may rest satisfied that absolutely no other blocks exist than the hundred and thirty-five now reunited in the Imperial Library.

The proof that the work is incomplete must be sought in the tablets and bandrols which, destined to inclose the inscriptions, are blank and print black, as may be seen in the engravings 130 to 135, and at the top of the banners in the engraving No. 57, &c. Another proof which may be adduced is the marking of the years at the back of the blocks, which, beginning at 1516, end at 1519, and leave scarcely any doubt that the work had been,stopped by the death of the Emperor, which took place in this same year, 1519. The suggestion of Sandrart, that these blocks had perished in a fire at Augsburg, becomes value-less in the fact of their actual existence ; and the facts mentioned above .will not allow us to refer this loss to another part of the blocks, as there is not the slightest proof that, besides those which are known, others have been engraved, and that they have been mislaid.*   If, however, any loss has taken place, it could only refer to two blocks at the most.

A small number of proofs were printed from some of these blocks, probably when first cut.   The Imperial Library possessed ninety of the oldest before there was any knowledge of the existence of the blocks.   Sandrart had only seen a hundred proofs ; Mariette possessed a set of eighty-seven pieces, according to the statement of Basan, who adds at the same time, in a note, that the cabinet of the king of Sweden held the like.   Impressions were taken from the blocks found at Ambras ; likewise some proofs were taken from those which had been at Gratz.   But these proofs having been. struck off in dif-ferent places, and in very small number, there was scarcely any means of obtaining them, supposing that any one desired to possess them in their then state ; viz., printed mostly in a negligent manner, and on common paper and of various kinds.

These considerations have led to the determination to publish this collection in a complete form, arranged in the prescribed order, printed with the necessary care, and accompanied with an explanatory text.

These blocks were engraved, as has been already said, in the years 1516, 1517, 1518, and 1519, by seventeen skilful wood-cutters, on the drawings of Hans (Jean) Burg-mair, painter, and pupil of Albert Durer, whose monogram H B is marked on many of the pieces.   The blocks are

---

* See Passavant's remarks on missing blocks. —ED.

of pear-wood, and the names of the engravers are written in full, in ink, on the back of a great number of them, or only engraved in monograms on the wood. They are :—

1. Jérôme André, properly named Resch or Rösch, and was in his time one of the most skilful wood-engravers of Nuremberg.*

2. Jean de Bonn. Papillon mentions a Bartholomé and a Corneille de Bonn.† This Jean is unknown.

3. Cornelius. According to probability, the same Corneille de Bonn whom we have named, or Corneille Liefrink, who follows at No. 7.

4. Hans Frank.

5. Saint German.

6. Guillaume. This is perhaps Liefrink, at No. 8.

7. Corneille Liefrink.

8. Guillaume Liefrink. A Jean Liefrink is known and mentioned by different authors, but we do not find any trace of a Guillaume.

9. Alexis Lindt.

10. Josse de Negkher, undersigned, wood-engraver at Augsburg, on many other pieces. He is noticed by Papillon,‡ who, however, only knew one other engraving of his. In the Imperial Library there are many other examples marked H B, and bearing at the same time the name of this engraver.§

11. Vincent Pfarkecher.

12. Jaques Rupp.

13. Hans Schaufelein de Nordlingen, a well-known artist, known by many wood-engravings, chiefly by those of Thuerdanck.‖

---

* C. T. Murr, "Journal zur Kunstgeschichte," &c., vol. ii. p. 158.
† "Traité de la Gravure en bois," vol. i. p. 135.
‡ Vol. i. p. 391.　　　　§ See Passavant, &c.—ED.
‖ The Theurdanck is an early and by no means a favourable specimen of the artist. See further notice of him.—ED.

14. Jean Taberith.

15. F. P.

16. ⱧⱣ meaning perhaps Hans Frank, named above, at No. 4.

17. W. R.

The statement of C. T. Murr* to the effect that it was Albert Durer who made the designs of this Triumph, for which the Emperor paid him a hundred florins a year, is by no means authentic, and appears to be only a conjecture of this writer. The letter of Albert Durer found in his journal, and in which there is mention of a Triumph, proves only that this artist had a claim of a hundred florins, but no mention is made of an annual salary. If the claim of a hundred florins, which might refer to the Triumphal Arch, which is one of the principal wood-engravings of Albert Durer, has special reference to this Triumph, it is evident that the interest which Durer had in it relates solely to the engravings, either entire or in part, which were engraved under his direction, possibly only by his engravers, who were stated to have lived and worked in his house. If Durer had made the designs, he would certainly have put his monogram on them, as he nearly always did on the wood-engravings designed by him.

An absolute proof that Burgmair is the designer, and not simply the engraver, as de Murr suggests in this very instance, is that the names of the engravers are written on the backs of the blocks, even of those where the monogram of Hans Burgmair appears on the woodcut.

This last speciality is very interesting, because it confirms at the same time this fact, which on many grounds we have no reason to doubt, that the monogram marked on a wood-engraving indicates nearly always the name of the designer, very rarely that of the engraver, except in the special instance where an engraver's tool is marked with the letters.

The engravings of the Triumph, far from being servile copies of the miniature paintings, differ entirely in style and design. Nearly all the groups have a different arrangement, each figure has a different pose ; Hans Burgmair appears before us rather in the character of an author than a copyist, more especially as he has surpassed his model in many points. But whatever may be the difference between the engravings and the drawings on vellum, the subjects still so far correspond, that they may be recognized without the least difficulty.

However, we must make an exception as regards eighteen plates, where this correspondence will be sought in vain ; viz. those twelve from No. 89 to 100, and six from 130 to 135. Of these we know nothing, except that they represent wars, and we have no means of naming them, as they have no resemblance to those in the painted one, and the search will be in vain for any proper mark to distinguish their true meaning, excepting No. 89, which we recognize as the Venetian war, by the lion ; and three others, where the heraldic shields may lead us to conjectures. It has been thought better to place these twelve engravings together, arranging them indistinctly but in a continuous line. The six others, whose subjects are entirely foreign to those of the painted leaves, appear to have been additions made during the course of the execution of the Triumph. The impossibility of assigning them an exact place has led to their being placed at the end of the work.*

To contribute as much as possible to the lustre of this work, care has been taken to deepen the places intended for the inscriptions, wherever it was apparent that the black masses would be too great, and might injure the delicacy and harmony of the engraving.†

* See the letter of the keeper of the Imperial Library.—ED.
† In our reproduction we have carried this plan throughout the series, as there was no engraving not injured in effect by the black mass on the scroll. —ED.

As regards the ancient description placed before them, the Imperial Library keeps two manuscripts. One is the first scheme, dictated in 1512 by the Emperor to his secretary Marc Treitzsaurwein, after which the Triumph was to be finished in painting.* The couplets are not here, only the theme written in prose. The other manuscript was written after the completion of the paintings in miniature. This contains all the couplets,† but the subjects have less detail than the prose, agreeing, however, in all things, except that the notice of the original project of the Triumph is omitted. It is from these two manuscripts that the description of the plates is drawn; the text of the former, which is more in detail, serves as a basis, and such information as may be gathered from the couplets is added. To distinguish the two texts interlaced in this style, the couplets are marked with a parenthesis, as also are all the variations or additions which are taken from the second manuscript, and which seem to be useful in rendering more clear the explanation of the engravings.

Such special care has been taken to preserve the original text in its integrity, that the names of a few subjects not mentioned in the manuscripts have been printed in a different character.

To render the reference to this description more easy and more general, the old German text is accompanied with a French translation. The couplets have been omitted, with the object of rendering it less tiresome,

---

* This manuscript does not differ from that which Murr has printed in the ninth volume of his "Journal," except in a few insignificant expressions. It should be noted that this last is not the rough copy written by the Emperor's own hand, as de Murr pretends, but a fair copy in a strange though cotemporary hand. It is now in the Imperial Library.

† Except eight, which have been extracted from a manuscript note-book, which has for its title "Vers zu Kayser Maximilian des ersten dis namens Triumph, 1512. Selbe mundlitch seiner kaj Mr. Secretarj Treizsaurwein angeben;" that is to say, "Verses for the Triumph of the Emperor Maximilian I. of this name, dictated in 1512 to Treizsaurwein, Secretary to his Majesty." This manuscript is the first rough copy, and the same from which Mr. de Murr made his copy in 1760 at Inspruck, afterwards placed in the Imperial Library.

without any risk of altering the essence of the original. These couplets, of which the substance is given, contain nothing but eulogiums on the Emperor, and are utterly devoid of historic or poetic interest. Robbed of their rhyme, which is their only merit, a translation would only have offered an insipid and disgusting verbiage.

THE TRIUMPH

OF THE

EMPEROR MAXIMILIAN I.

OF GLORIOUS MEMORY.

Translated from the Preface of 1796.

THAT which is written in this book has been dictated by the Emperor Maximilian to me, Marc Treitzsaurwein, Secretary to his Majesty, in the year 1512.

In the sequel follows the order according to which the "Triumph" of the Emperor Maximilian must be arranged and painted.

———o———

PRECO (HERALD OF THE TRIUMPH).

PL. 1. The march commences with a naked man mounted on a griffin (an imaginary animal) without a saddle. The wings of the animal partially cover the man. He holds in his mouth a twisted horn of peculiar form. He bears the name of Preco, and is decorated with a crown of honour.

REPRESENTATION OF THE TITLES.

PL. 2. Two horses harnessed into shafts, led by two grooms, and carrying a large board, on which is placed a large tablet ornamented à l'Italienne, on which are written the following titles.

TITLES OF THE EMPEROR.

This Triumph has been executed in praise of and for the perpetual commemoration of the noble pursuits and glorious victories of his most serene and very illustrious Prince and Lord Maximilian, Roman Emperor elect and chief of Christendom, king and heir of seven Christian kingdoms, Archduke of Austria, Duke of Burgundy, and of other grand principalities and provinces of Europe, &c.

FIFES AND DRUMS.

PL. 3. The fifer Anthony (of Dornstädt) mounted on horseback and bearing his couplet. He is distinguished from the other fifers by his dress. He carries by his side the case of his instrument and a long sabre. The substance of his couplet is nearly as follows :—" I, Anthony of Dornstädt, have played the fife in many countries for the valorous Emperor Maximilian in many great battles, also in tourneys, both friendly and hostile. For these services I have the honour of appearing in my rank of fifer in this Triumph."

Following are three mounted fifers playing their instruments. They are clad in coats of arms (in the ancient fashion, their heads covered with little blue hats ornamented with plumes). They carry instrument-cases and wear long sabres.

PL. 4. Five mounted drummers marching in line and beating their drums. They are clad in the ancient fashion, and have long sabres at their sides.

All the fifers and drummers are decorated with the crown of honour.

FALCONRY.

PL. 5. Hans Teuschel, master falconer, mounted on horseback, and clad in a hunting coat of more distinguished fashion than those worn by his followers. He has his hawking-pouch by his side, and bears his couplet, which says in substance that, profiting by the instruction of the Emperor, he has carried falconry to such perfection that he is ready to afford his master the pleasures of the chase, both in winter and summer.

PL. 6. Following on horseback, and in line, are five falconers, of whom four carry a hawk perched on the fist, and the fifth an owl.* They are clad as falconers, and have their pouches attached. One carries a wand.

All the falconers are decorated with the crown of honour.

Below them, in the air, are three hawks, one chasing a heron, the second a vulture, and the third a duck.

WILD-GOAT AND CHAMOIS HUNT.

PL. 7. A chamois-hunter, in the costume of his calling.

This hunter is Conrad Zuberle. He bears his couplet, which implies that he has carried out the perilous chase of the wild goat and the chamois, according to the suggestions furnished to him by the Emperor, in a more diverting manner than had hitherto been known.

Following these, five wild goats and chamois in line, and intermixed.

PL. 8. Five chamois-hunters clad in doublet and breeches, shod with high shoes,[1] and carrying their crampirons,[2] havre-sacs,[3] knives, snow-hoops,[4] and staves. The latter are pointed below, and furnished at the top with a cutting-blade.

All the chamois-hunters are decorated with the crown of honour.

* See Observations on Plates.—ED.
[1] Shoes that are tied above the ankle-bone, to exclude small stones detached in climbing.
[2] Iron hooks, which the hunter fastens on to his soles with leather bands, to prevent his slipping whilst mounting steep rocks or places slippery from snow or ice.
[3] The chamois inhabit only the highest and most desert mountains, whose summit is bald. The approach is as difficult as it is long, and the hunters are obliged to take provisions for several days, which they carry in havresacs, and which are ordinarily composed of bread, cheese, and a mixture of melted butter and flour.
[4] We see in the engraving these snow-hoops slung from the thighs of the hunters. The thin hoop has many bands of leather interlaced, to form the bottom. The hunter attaches it below the sole of his shoes, and thus saves himself from the danger of sinking in snowdrifts.

R

STAG-HUNT.

PL. 9. Conrad von Rot, master of the staghounds, on horseback, and carrying his couplet. He is clad in a dress which distinguishes him from the other hunters. (It is of an ancient fashion.) He carries a hunting-horn of the Low Countries. His couplet says that he has arranged the · chase of the stag according to the suggestions of the Emperor, both in the mountains and the plains, in a manner to give everybody great pleasure.

Five stags marching abreast.

PL. 10. Five hunters follow, mounted and abreast (in ancient dresses), with their hunting-knives by their sides, carrying the hunting-horns of the Low Countries, and holding staves in their hands.

All the hunters are decorated with the crown of honour.·

WILD-BOAR HUNT.

PL. 11. Wilhelm von Greyssen,[5] master hunter of the wild boar, on horseback, bearing his couplet. He is distinguished by his dress from the others, &c. The couplet, in substance, states that, following the directions of the Emperor, he has arranged the chase in such a manner as to give the greatest satisfaction.

Five furious wild boars represented marching.

PL. 12. After them five mounted wild-boar hunters, carrying their new swords and their naked spears. Each carries a German hunting-horn.

These hunters are decorated with the crown of honour.

BEAR-HUNT.

PL. 13. Theobold von Schlandersberg, master hunter of bears, mounted, well clothed according to his position, carrying a large hunting-horn and displaying his couplet,

---

[5] This Wilhelm von Greyssen is the writer of a treatise upon hunting which has never been printed, but exists in manuscript in the Imperial library.

which expresses that, following the information given
by the Emperor, he has planned the perilous bear-hunt
in a new and strange manner, calculated to afford fine
sport.

Five bears abreast, some turning their heads, and threatening the hunters who are behind them.

Pl. 14. Five bear-hunters follow on foot. They have short coats
and girdles. Each carries a hunting-knife and a spear.
The bear-hunters are decorated with the crown of honour.

THE FIVE OFFICES OF THE COURT.

Pl. 15. Following the hunt is a man on horseback carrying a
tablet on which is inscribed the five offices of the
Court; viz. those of the cupbearer, the cook, the
barber, the tailor, and the shoemaker.[6] It is Eber-
bach, vice-marshal, who carries the tablet. His couplet
is not yet written.[7]

Pl. 16. Five men on horseback and in line. The first carries
a goblet, the second a ladle, the third a razor, the
fourth a tailor's scissors, the fifth a last.
All decorated with the crown of honour.

MUSIC OF THE LUTE AND REBEC.[8]

Pl. 17, A low car with plough wheels, drawn by two elks and
18.   driven by a young boy, who carries at the same time

[6] It appears to have been the duty of these five officers to be in constant
personal attendance on the Emperor, because their services were absolutely
necessary. For this reason he could not omit them in this "Triumph." In
a manuscript which contains the history of the captivity of the Emperor Maximilian at Bruges, given with much detail, we find amongst the Imperial
attendants the names of Michel Raphael, equerry to his majesty; Spreng, the
cupbearer; Master George, the cook; Abert, the harness-keeper; Graff, the
barber. The only officer wanting is the shoemaker. It does not appear that
these officers, except the two first, were attached to the Court, either before or
after Maximilian.

[7] The reader must remember, that on this and other occasions it is the
Emperor who speaks whilst arranging the work.

[8] An ancient word, which signifies a violin with three strings and tuned in
fifths. It is derived from a Spanish word, *Rabel*, in Arabic *Rebab*, which the
Italians have made into *Ribeba*. The rebec is our present violincello, as may
be distinctly seen in the woodcut. (See Observations on Plates.—Ed.)

the couplet. In the car are seated five players of lute and rebec. At their head is Artus, master player of the lute, and his couplet states that with the assistance of the Emperor he has brought to perfection the music of the lute and rebec.

The musicians and the boy-driver are decorated with the crown of honour.

MUSIC OF THE PIPES, TROMBONES, AND TRUMPETS.

PL. 19, 20. Another low car with plough wheels, drawn by two buffaloes and driven by a little boy, who carries the master's couplet. In the car are seated five musicians. Neyschl, trombone master, is at their head. His couplet, carried by the young driver, expresses that he has brought this sort of music to perfection under the instructions of the Emperor.

The musicians and the little boy are decorated with the crown of honour.

MUSIC OF THE REGAL[9] AND POSITIF.*

PL. 21, 22. A car similar to the last, drawn by a camel and driven by a little boy, who carries the master's couplet. On this car is a regal and a positif. Paul Hofhaimer,[10] master organist, is playing the latter instrument. His couplet contains, in substance, that by the aid of the Emperor he has learnt and brought to perfection this kind of music.

These musicians and the little boy are decorated with the crown of honour.

[9] According to Cuspinien, this instrument was invented during the reign of Maximilian I.—Diarium apud M. Freheri, "Script. Rer. Austr.," vol. ii. p. 607.
* The positif was a choir organ.—ED.
[10] He was born at Salsburg, and was court organist to Maximilian I. Ottomarus Luscinius speaks of him in high terms.—Musurg, lib. i. p. 15. Cuspinien calls him the king of musicians and the first organist of Germany.— Diarium, p. 607. His poetic harmonies were printed at Nuremberg in 1539.

MUSIC OF SWEET MELODY.

PL. 23, A car similar to the last, drawn by a dromedary and
24.   driven by a little boy, who carries the master's couplet.
         After follows sweet melody, given by the following instru-
         ments : a drum, a quinterne,[11] a great lute, a rebec, a
         violin, a loud flute,[12] a harp, and a large loud flute.

The master of the music has not been named, and his couplet
has not yet been written.

The musicians and the boy driving are decorated with the
crown of honour.

MUSIC OF THE KAPELLA.

PL. 25, A similar little car on plough wheels, drawn by two bisons
26.   and driven by a little boy, who carries the couplet of
         . the Kapelmeister. In this car is the orchestra and
         some cornet- and trombone-players. Herr George
         Slakony,[13] Bishop of Vienna, is the master of the
         Kapella, and his couplet signifies that he has arranged
         the singing of the kapella in the most agreeable
         manner, under the instructions of the Emperor. Steudl
         is the master of the trombones, and Augustin is the
         cornet-master. A little boy, seated in the car, carries
         their couplet, which certifies that they have brought to
         perfection the consonance of the cornets and trom-
         bones, following the advice of the Emperor.

The little boy and all these musicians are decorated with the
crown of honour.

JESTERS.

PL. 27. Conrad von der Rosen[14] on horseback, dressed as
         a jester, and carrying the couplet of jesters and
         fools.

This couplet is not yet written.

[11] A musical instrument with four or five catgut strings. The body is
elongated, like a guitar. Draudius, in his "Bibliotheca Classica," p. 1625,
mentions a Latin work which treats of the manner of playing this instrument.
[12] This flute, since improved, is now called the hautboy.
[13] Bishop of Vienna, and confidential adviser of the Emperor. His arms
are emblazoned on the car near him.
[14] This Conrad von der Rosen was a court jester and the confidant of the
Emperor. His courage was equal to his strength, and he saved the life of

PL. 28. A small car drawn by two wild horses, in which are seated the following buffoons : Lenz, Caspar, Bauer, Meterschy, and Dyweyndl.

A little boy drives them, and they are all decorated with the crown of honour.

FOOLS.

PL. 29, Another small car, containing the following fools :
30. Gylyme, Bock, Gulichisch, Caspar, Hans Wynter, Guggeryllis. It is drawn by a mule (by two asses), and driven by a little boy.

The jesters and natural fools, as also the two little drivers, are decorated with the crown of honour.

MUMMERY.

PL. 31, Herr Peter von Altenhaus, master of mummery, mounted,
32. and handsomely clad in the coat of the golden masque. He carries his couplet, which states that under the orders of the Emperor he has arranged mummery in an amusing manner.

Following are two ranks of masked men on foot, each rank consisting of five men, and each man carrying a lighted torch. The first rank is the Golden mummery. The maskers wear the short dress of the ancient Suabians.

The second rank represents Spanish mummery. The maskers have short golden coats mixed with colour, and with slashed and flying sleeves.

All these persons are decorated with the crown of honour.

---

his master, at the peril of his own, on various occasions. Fugger relates several anecdotes of this remarkable man in his history, entitled "Spiegel der Ehren" ("Mirror of Honour"), and he notices his exploits at greater length in his geat work, named "Ehrenwerk" ("Book of Honour"), of which the manuscript is in the Imperial library. In the latter is his portrait in minia-ture, from an original painting, which, at the time when Fugger lived, was seen at Augsburg. It is a half-length, full face, the left hand grasping a big sword. The portrait of a German knight, represented in the attitude which we have described, and engraved by David Hopfer, is this same Conrad von der Rosen.

FENCING.

PL. 33. Herr Hans Hollywars,[15] fencing-master, on horseback, and clad in regulation style. He carries his couplet, signifying that, following the suggestions of the Emperor, he has arranged the noble art of fencing at the Court.

Following the fencers, marching on foot in ranks of five men, we have :—

Five men with leathern flails.

PL. 34. Five men with short staves.

PL. 35. Five men with lances.

PL. 36. Five men with halberds.

Five men with battle-axes.

PL. 37. Five men with shields, carrying the sword drawn (with fencing-swords and hand-shields).

PL. 38. Five men with little targes and naked knives (swords—ED.).

PL. 39. Five men (in Hungarian costume) with pavois[16] (Hungarian targes) and Hungarian military maces (iron maces).

PL. 40. Five men with sabres (ordinary two-handed swords), which they carry over their shoulders.

All these persons are decorated with the crown of honour.

TOURNEY.[17]

PL. 41. Herr Anthony von Yfan, master of tourney, mounted, in complete armour, as for the tourney, and carrying his

---

[15] This, according to appearances, is the Holubar, known by a fight which took place between him and Matthias, king of Hungary.—Galeotti, "Comment. de dictis et factis Mathiæ Regis, cap. 14. Apud Schwandtneri Script. Rer. Hung.," vol. i. pl. 2, p. 545.

[16] A kind of shield invented by Ziska. The name is derived from the word *pawesa*, which, in the Bohemian tongue, signifies shield.

[17] We owe the possibility of rendering this chapter, and the explanations which accompany it, almost entirely to two manuscripts enriched with figures painted in colours, which are in the Imperial library, and in which are seen

couplet, stating that he has arranged the tourney in a manner worthy of the grandeur of the court of the Emperor, and following his instructions.

PL. 42. A row of five tilters on foot, completely ·armed, their heads covered with the casque,[18] and not with the heaume.[19] They wear the sword and the lances of horsemen, as jousters do, but their lances are without guards.[20]

PL. 43. A rank of five tilters, mounted, completely armed, wearing swords and horsemen's lances, the head protected by a casque.

All these persons wear the crown of honour over the casque.

the representations and the names of all the kinds of tournaments which are found in the plates of this Triumph. Jeremy Schemel is the author of one of these manuscripts. He was a painter at Augsburg, about the year 1570 : the other, shorter and by an unknown author, but apparently written in the time of the Emperor Maximilian, has for its title, "Etliche Rennen und Treffen Kaisers Maximilians I." The first, which is the most instructive, contains exact copies of the plates of this Triumph, accompanied with the names of each kind of joust and course, and explanations of the armour of the knights and the equipment of their horses. Although these explanations are not as complete as we could desire, they furnish nevertheless, on many points, useful information, and the more precious, that we cannot find them in any other authors who have treated of ancient tourney. It is entirely owing to these two manuscripts that it is possible to arrange the plates of these tourneys according to their respective names.

[18] They had casques of different shapes and different names. For example, they call *Alte Helmlin* the small ancient casques, or *Alte Stechhelme*, ancient tourney casques, those which we see in Plates 42, 43, 45, 46, 47, 48; *Neue Stechhelme*, the modern tourney casques, in Plate 49 ; *Rennhüte* or *Eisenhüte*, tilting-caps or head-pieces, those in Plates 50, 51, 52, and 55. Thus we see the French had formerly their *morions, bassinets, salades, cabassets, armets, pots*, and *burgonets*, of which we can only say that they designate different kinds of casques, but the exact meaning of which is lost with the things themselves. (See Observations on Plates.—ED.)

[19] The heaume was of entirely different shape from those mentioned in the preceding note. The opening for the eyes was furnished with a grating or barred work, which served for a vizor. We see these heaumes in nearly all ancient armories, but they were no longer in use in Maximilian's time.

[20] The vamplate is to the lance what the guard is to the sword, that is to say, a round or semicircular protruding piece, able to ward off the stroke of an adversary's lance. They called these vamplates Scheiben, Brechscheiben, that is to say, rings or guardrings, when they were circular ; Schwebscheiben, that is to say, movable vamplates, when they were semicircular. This form is also described by the term Gärbeisen, drayoire, probably from their resemblance to the tanner's head-knife, which bears the same name.

JOUSTS.[21]

PL. 44. Herr Wolfgang von Polheim, master of jousts and of the course, mounted and clad as a tilter. His head is unarmed, only wearing the crown of honour. He has a golden chain round his neck, and bears no target. He carries his couplet, stating that the games of chivalry have never been exercised in the world with the same varieties of style as in the court of the Emperor, where they have been instituted with his assistance.

Here follow the jousts and the tilting.

PL. 45. The Italian joust, a rank of five men.

PL. 46. The German joust, a rank of five men.

PL. 47. The joust with the high poitrel,[22] a rank of five men.

PL. 48. The joust with leg armour, a rank of five men ; the horses caparisoned with leather.

The jousters carry their lances high and hold them below the vamplate. They are decorated with the crown of honour, and each bears his crest on his casque.[23]

---

[21] The joust is properly the single combat with the lance, and is distinguished from the tourney, which is an encounter between several knights, who fight in a troop.

It is to be observed here, that in the place of jousts and tiltings specified hereafter, the second manuscript describing the Triumph, painted in miniature, says only, "Several rows of jousters and tilters, each of five men, follow."

[22] The jousters of this kind were seated on a very high saddle, before the pommel of which was raised a heurt, also very high. It is called heurt (from heurter), in German Vorbug, that part of the iron armour which the tourney horse carries before his chest. This saddle and this heurt, taken together, were named in German hohes Zeug, that is to say, high barde. The designs for this furniture are found in the manuscript *Etliche Rennen*, &c. We see from that, that G. Schubart was in error when he imagined that the German name for this kind of joust came from the long lances they employed.—De Ludis equestribus. Halæ, 1725.

[23] These crests are only seen in the German joust.

COURSES.[24]

PL. 49. The Italian course, with mornettes.[25] These are rounded, and have round vamplates,[26] a rank of five men.

PL. 50. The course named Bund,[27] a rank of five men with the targes,[28] which fly over their heads.

PL. 51. The course of the ingenious breastplate,[29] a rank of five men with breastplates, of which the pieces leap into the air.

The Elmet (*Helmlet*) course,[30] a rank of five men.[31]

[24] The difference between the joust and the course consisted in this, that in the latter the lances were pointed with iron, in the former they were tipped with three hooks placed in a triangle. This iron was named in Germany *Krönlein*, or little crown. The armour of the champions and the poitrel of the horses were much lighter in the courses than in the jousts, and it seems that the rush of the horses and the stroke of the lance were delivered with much more rapidity.

[25] A species of lance, which the combatants protected with a case of iron, so as not to wound the adversary. These protectors are not noticed in the plates.

[26] The Emperor made this remark on purpose to distinguish the different kinds of arm-guard. All, except two, have drayoires for arm-guards in the following courses.

[27] The representation of this course exactly corresponds with that given in the manuscript by Schemel, and which has this inscription in German : "This course is called Bund"; but there is no characteristic which throws any light on this name. The word Bund has various meanings ; as union, association, bundle of sticks, truss, packet.

[28] It was upon these targes that the jousters, to apply the terms then in use, gave and received the strokes ; and as they were but lightly attached, they flew into the air when the stroke was good. These targes bore also the name of chapeau de mentonnière or grande mentonnière. (See Note 34.)

[29] It appears that the targes which were used in this kind of course were arranged so that the springs, united in the centre, held the different pieces ingeniously together ; but when struck on the union of the springs, the pieces flew up.

[30] The word *elmet* has the same origin as the German *Helmlet*, the Italian *Elmétto*, which signified formerly in Italy a kind of little helmet.—"Diction. de Trevoux," article Armet ; and "Dizion. della Crusca," article Elmetto.

[31] We cannot avoid remarking that this kind of course, as well as the three others, of which there are no engravings, is neither found in the work of Schemel, nor in the MS. entitled "Etliche Rennen," &c. Is it not possible that one kind of course might have two different names, and that the names

PL. 52. The Shield course,[32] a rank of five men with movable vamplates,[33] and chapeaux à la mentonnière.[34]

PL. 53. The Breastplate course,[35] a rank of five men.

The course in the Gaspar Wintzer style,[36] a rank of five men, carrying targes and drayoires.

The Vamplate course, a rank of five men with elmets.

PL. 54. The Camp course, a rank of five men with round guards and small targes.

PL. 55. *The course à la queue (schweifrennen).* *

PL. 56. *The course with the wreath.*[37]

of the two latter courses, newly inserted, relate to two of the four without engravings? Is it not probable that the majority of these names were the creation of the Emperor? The jousts and courses, taken together, occupy twelve engravings. There is one more amongst the miniatures, but as it bears no inscription, we cannot determine to which of the four mentioned names it relates.

[32] Named also the course of the ingenious shield (Geschäftet-Scheiben-Rennen). It was on this shield that the assault was delivered. (See Note 29.)

[33] See Note 20.

[34] They called the mentonnière the lower part of the casque, which covers the chin, the neck, and half of the chest. The chapeau de mentonnière, also called the great mentonnière, was a kind of shield which the champion attached above the mentonnière, or, if he had it not, simply on the chin. To have the chapeau à la mentonnière was as much as to say, to be armed with this targe. These chapeaux differed from the mentonnière in that they were larger. Usually they were ornamented with the same material as the caparison of the horse.

[35] The stroke was delivered on a breastplate, which the tilter wore attached to his chest. It consisted of a square piece of wood surrounded by a border and ornamented with embossed work. In place of this it was sometimes covered with open iron-work, which they called simply the *Gril* (Rost). As the champions fought with bare heads, and were only armed with a cuirass, this kind of course was extremely perilous. It was their custom to place a coffin in the tilting-ground before the champions undertook the course.

[36] This Gaspar Wintzer is mentioned by Fugger amongst the combatants in a tourney given by Maximilian at Vienna in 1515, in the place called Am Hofe.—"Ehrenspiegel," p. 1335.

* See Observations on the Plates.—ED.

[37] In ancient times knights of a certain class wore their casques ornamented with a wreath, which most commonly was composed of the colours of their mistress.—Wilson de la Colombière, "Science héroïque," p. 416. (See Observations on the Plates.—ED.)

The tilters carry their lances high, holding them above the drayoires.[38]

They are all in appropriate costume, and decorated with the crown of honour.

THE MARRIAGE OF BURGUNDY.

Three kettle-drummers in the Austrian livery.

Two ranks of five trumpeters in the Austrian livery.

They are decorated with the crown of honour.

THE HEREDITARY COUNTRIES OF THE HOUSE OF AUSTRIA.

The hereditary countries of the house of Austria are represented on standards, and not on gonfalons, with their shields, helmets, and crests. The standards of the countries in which the Emperor has made war are borne by the cuirassed horsemen. The armour of each is variously designed after the ancient form. Those of the horsemen in whose countries the Emperor has not made war are magnificently clad, each according to the fashion of his country, and they are all decorated with the crown of honour.

PL. 57. Austria.
 The ancient arms of Austria.
 Styria.

PL. 58. Carinthia, Carniola, Swabia.

PL. 59. Alsace, Hapsburg, Tyrol.

PL. 60. Goritz, Ferreten, Kyburg.

PL. 61. The Countries on the Ens, Burgau, Cilley.

PL. 62. Nellenburg, Hohenberg, Seckingen and Urach.

PL. 63. Glaris, Sonnenberg, Feldkirch.

PL. 64. Ortenburg, Ehingen, Achalm.

[38] The champions of the Italian course only hold the hand below the vamplates, which are circular.

PL. 65. Friburg, Bregentz, Saulgau.

PL. 66. Waldhausen, Ravensburg, Kirchberg.

PL. 67. Tockenburg, Andex, Frioul.

PL. 68. Trieste, Windismark, Pordenone.

PL. 69. Triberg, Rhatzuns or Razins, Torgau.

PL. 70. Reineck, the grey league of the Grisons, Lieben.

PL. 71. Ehrenberg, Weissenhorn, Hohenstauffen.

PL. 72. Rapperswyl, the Black Forest, Neuburg on the Inn.

PL. 73. Tybein or Duino, Upper Waldsee, *Lower Waldsee.*

PL. 74. Burgundy, Zeringen.

PL. 75. Bohemia, heritage ; England, heritage.

PL. 76. *Portugal, heritage;* Moravia, heritage.

BURGUNDIAN FIFERS.

PL. 77 to 79. Burgundian fifers playing on the bombarde[20] and the loud flute. They are decorated with the crown of honour.

THE PROVINCES OF BURGUNDY.

The provinces of Burgundy, represented on standards borne by horsemen. They wear no cuirass, but are magnificently clad, and carry precious chains round the neck.

PL. 80. Burgundy (the duchy), Lorraine, Brabant.

PL. 81. Limburg, Luxemburg, Gueldres.

PL. 82. Hainalt, Burgundy (Franche Comté, or Upper Burgundy), Flanders, Artois, Holland, Zealand.

PL. 83. Namur, Zutphen, Friesland.

PL. 84. Malines, Salins, Antwerp.

PL. 85. Charolois, Maconois, Auxerrois.

PL. 86. Boulogne, Alost, Chimay.

---

[20] A bass instrument, which formerly served to accompany the fifes. Its name came from an Italian word, *bombare,* to hum.

PL. 87. Ostrevant, Arco, Aussone.

PL. 88. Tenremonde, Franeker, Bethune.

THE MARRIAGE OF THE EMPEROR.

Two men on horseback carry the marriage of the Emperor, entitled "The Marriage of the Emperor Maximilian to the hereditary Princess of Burgundy."

VICTORIES AND CONQUESTS.

PL. 89 Some lansquenets[40] in Roman costume, carrying castles
to 100.   and towns.

WAR IN HAINAULT.

Some lansquenets carrying the war of Hainault; with this inscription, "The war in Hainault and Picardy."

BATTLE NEAR TERROUANE.

Some lansquenets carrying the battle of Terrouane; with this inscription, "Battle near Terrouane, in Artois."

FIRST WAR OF GUELDRES.

Some lansquenets carrying the first war of Gueldres; with this inscription, "The first conquest of Gueldres."

WAR OF UTRECHT.

Some lansquenets carrying the war of Utrecht; entitled "The war of Utrecht."

FIRST WAR IN FLANDERS.

Some lansquenets carrying the first war in Flanders; thus entitled, "The first conquest of Flanders."

---

[40] The lansquenets were soldiers engaged for the term of a campaign, and who served both within and outside the empire. They were instituted and drilled by Maximilian I. They were the first regular troops of which we have any knowledge in the history of Germany.—Fugger, p. 1372.

WAR OF LIEGE.

Some lansquenets carrying the war of Liege; entitled, "The victory obtained over the people of Liege."

TROPHY CAR.

Pl. 101, A car with a trophy, composed of the different arms
102.   and armours of the Low Countries and of France; also standards of all kinds of colours.

(This car is preceded by a man on horseback.)

ROMAN CORONATION.

Two men on horseback, carrying a picture where is represented the coronation of the King of the Romans.

There is a shield with the double-headed eagle, and the inscription is, "The coronation of the Emperor as King of the Romans." The Roman empire is represented by a lady wearing the Imperial dress and the Imperial crown.

Three men in noble costume (of ancient fashion, and marching in single file) and carrying the three Roman crowns on their cushions; namely, (the first,) the crown of straw (crown of rue; the second,) the crown of iron (the Royal crown; and the third,) the crown of gold (the Imperial crown).

THE GERMAN EMPIRE.

A man mounted, and bearing the picture of the German empire, represented by the Emperor seated and clad in royal vestments as king of the Romans.

In the shield the eagle has only one head, such as belongs to a king of the Romans.

The three provinces of Austria, Bavaria, and Saxony, and the three bishoprics of Magdeburg, Salzburg, and Bremen, with their emblazoned shields.

The empire of Germany is represented by a lady with long hair, wearing a crown.

SECOND WAR IN FLANDERS.

Some lansquenets carrying the war in Flanders ; with this inscription, " The second conquest of provinces of Flanders."

WAR IN BURGUNDY. ·

Some lansquenets carrying the war in Burgundy; entitled,
" The conquest of the two counties of Burgundy and Artois."

AUSTRIAN WAR.

Some lansquenets carrying the Austrian war ; which has for its
title, " The conquest of a part of Lower Austria."

HUNGARIAN WAR.

Some lansquenets carrying the Hungarian war; with this in-
scription, " The bloody war in Hungary."
(After them, some horsemen bear the heraldic standards of
Dalmatia, Croatia, and Bosnia.)

TROPHY CAR OF HUNGARY.

A car with a trophy, composed of the different arms of
   Hungary, Poland, Turkey, and Illyria (and ornamented
   with four little banners).

MARRIAGE OF KING PHILIP.

Horsemen magnificently clad, with costly chains round their
   necks, carrying on their standards the arms of the kingdoms of Spain (Castile, Leon, Aragon, Sicily, Jerusalem,
   Naples, Granada, Toledo, Galicia, Valentia, Sardinia,
   Catalonia, Biscay, fifteen hundred islands).

Two men mounted, carrying the marriage of King Philip, with
   this inscription : " Marriage of King Philip, Archduke
   of Austria, son of the Emperor Maximilian, with the
   hereditary Princess of Spain."

Pl. 103. (In the picture is represented the Emperor Maximilian, King Philip and the Queen of Spain, in their imperial and royal decorations, each having their shield near them.)

SWISS WAR.

Some lansquenets carrying the Swiss war; entitled, "The horrible war with the Swiss."

NEAPOLITAN WAR.

Some lansquenets carrying the Neapolitan war; with this inscription, "Naples victoriously relieved."

BAVARIAN WAR.

Some lansquenets carrying the Bavarian war; entitled, "The Bavarian war."
(Some horsemen carrying on their standards the arms of Kuffstein, Rotenburg, and Kitzbuhel.)

BATTLE OF BOHEMIA.

Some lansquenets carrying the battle of Bohemia; with this inscription, "The battle of Bohemia."

TROPHY CAR OF BOHEMIA.

In the trophy car of Bohemia are found different arms, armours, shields, and banners of different colours.

SECOND WAR IN GUELDRES.

Some lansquenets carrying the second war of Gueldres; entitled, "The long second war in Gueldres."

RECAPTURE OF MILAN.

Some lansquenets carrying the recapture of Milan; with this inscription, "Milan reconquered."

T

VENETIAN WAR.

Some lansquenets carrying the Venetian war; with this inscription, "The long Venetian war."

ITALIAN TROPHY CAR.

A car with a trophy composed of the arms and standards of Lombardy.

FRONTISPIECE OF WARS.

A man on horseback carrying a tablet with a couplet, which contains in substance this—

In this Triumph are marked the countries conquered by the arms cf his Majesty.

The towns, forts, and castles taken by him are numberless, and the memory of man is incapable of retaining them.

(Two men carry the model of a little galley.

Two others carry that of a large galley.

Two others carry a large ship.

Four others carry a picture, on which is written, "Different naval wars finished at sea and in the rivers." In the same picture are also represented ships of different sizes on the water.)

THE KINGDOM OF LOMBARDY.

A horseman armed *cap-à-pie*, bearing a standard with the arms of the kingdom of Lombardy, with the following inscription, "The kingdom of Lower Lombardy."

THE SIX NEW AUSTRIAN AND BURGUNDIAN KINGDOMS.

Some horsemen carry on their standards the arms of the Archipalatinate, of the Archduchy, and of the kingdoms of Austrasia and of Lorraine, of Belgium, of Slavonia or the Wendes, of New Austrasia, and of Austria.[41]

---

[41] Many indications are found which lead to the belief that the Emperor Maximilian intended to elevate the archduchy of Austria into a kingdom, but

In these royal standards are represented the Roman empire, and the Austrian countries making part of the empire.

The standards are borne by horsemen magnificently attired.

ARTILLERY.

Here follows a park of artillery, having this title, "Famous artillery."

The persons who accompany it are decorated with the crown of honour.

TREASURE.

Four men carry the Imperial jewels and treasure; the title is, "The jewels and the treasure used by the Emperor."

The persons carrying them are decorated with the crown of honour.

TREASURE OF THE KAPELLA.

Four men carry the treasure of the kapella; with this inscription, "The treasure of the kapella."

The persons who carry it are decorated with the crown of honour.

SEPULCHRAL STATUES.

A man on horseback carrying a picture, on which is written: "The following statues represent the illustrious emperors, kings, archdukes, and dukes whose countries form part of the possessions of the Emperor, and whose arms he bears."

The horseman is decorated with the crown of honour.

These statues, of which each is accompanied by the heraldic shield of the prince it represents, are placed on poles carried by horses.

The grooms who lead the horses are decorated with the crown of honour.

---

it is doubtful with regard to the six other provinces, for which he announces here the same project of elevation. It remains still to be discovered which of the provinces he wished on this occasion to erect into an archipalatinate and into an archduchy.

These are the names of the sepulchral statues :—

The Emperor Frederick III. decorated with the Imperial ornaments.

The Emperor Charles in cuirass, and ornaments above it.

Rodolph, King of the Romans, in cuirass, and with the ornaments.

Albert I., King of the Romans, with the ornaments above the cuirass.

Albert the last, King of the Romans, without cuirass, only with ornaments.

King Arthur, in complete armour.

King Ladislaus, in royal costume of ancient fashion.

King Philip, clothed as Ladislaus.

King Etienne, in ancient royal costume.

King John of Portugal, in ancient costume.

The Archduke Frederick of Austria, clad as archduke and holding the archiducal sceptre.

The Archduke Sigismund of Austria, clad as archduke and holding the archiducal sceptre.

Duke Philip of Burgundy, in ducal robes.

Duke Charles of Burgundy, in ducal robes.

Madame Cunegonde, Duchess.

Madame Margaret, Duchess.

Madame Cymburga, Archduchess.

Madame Maria, Archduchess.

Elizabeth, Queen of the Romans.

Bianca Maria, Queen of the Romans.

Eleonora, Roman Empress.

Sepulchral statues following the order observed in the plates :[42]—

PL. 104. Frederick III.

[42] We have deemed it necessary to give here a second list of sepulchral statues, arranged according to the number and order observed in the plates, where we only find seventeen statues in place of twenty-one, and where there are some not marked in the first list. The names of these are taken from the miniature paintings, where the number of statues is thirty-three.

PL. 105. Charlemagne.
     Clovis I.
     Etienne, King of Hungary.
     Albert I.

PL. 106. *Odobert, King of Provence.*
     Arthur, King of England.
     John, King of Portugal.
     Godfrey de Bouillon, King of Jerusalem.

PL. 107. Albert, King of the Romans.
     Albert, King of the Romans, of Hungary, and Bohemia.
     Ladislaus, King of Hungary and of Bohemia.
     Ferdinand, King of Spain.

PL. 108. Philip, King of Castile.
     St. Leopold, Margrave of Austria.
     Sigismund, Archduke of Austria.
     Charles, Duke of Burgundy.

PRISONERS.

(A man on horseback, carrying a tablet, on which is written, "The prisoners of different nations whom the Emperor has conquered.")

PL. 109, Two groups of prisoners (of different nations), surrounded
110.   by a chain and escorted by some lansquenets.

All the lansquenets appearing in this Triumph, without a single exception, wear the doublet and military hose, and are decorated with the crown of honour.

All the horsemen represented in this Triumph, also without exception, are decorated with the crown of honour.

PL. 111, Two groups of ten men, each carrying a statue of a
112.   female figure winged, and carrying a palm-branch in her hand.[43]

[43] It is probable that these little statues represent treaties of peace and alliances concluded by Maximilian I.

IMPERIAL TRUMPETERS.

Pl. 113 A large number of mounted trumpeters and kettle-
to 115. drummers, having the Imperial arms figured on the
streamers of their instruments.

All decorated with the crown of honour.

HERALDS.

Pl. 116 Some mounted heralds clad in their coats (marked by
to 118. different devices, and each carrying a yellow wand).

They are all decorated with the crown of honour.

IMPERIAL STANDARD.

Christopher Schenk, mounted, cuirassed, decorated with
the crown of honour, and bearing the standard of the
empire, with the double-headed eagle.

THE SWORD OF THE EMPIRE.

The Marshal of the empire carrying the sword of the
empire.

He is magnificently clad, and decorated with the crown of
honour.

TRIUMPHAL CAR OF THE EMPEROR.

The triumphal car of the Emperor is magnificently con-
structed. On it is seated, in all his majesty, the
Emperor in his Imperial robes. On this car, according to their ranks, are seated his first wife, Philip
and his wife and Frau Margaret, and King Philip's
children. The Archduke Charles crowned.*

This car is drawn by horses equipped in splendid harness,
becoming a car of Imperial triumph.

---

* There is an error in the French translation, which has been corrected
from the German.—Ed.

PRINCES.[44]

A horseman in magnificent costume and decorated with the
crown of honour, carrying a tablet, on which is written,
"The elected princes." The princes mounted in ranks
of five, carrying their banners, on which their names are
written.

> Frederic, Duke of Saxony.
> Albert, Duke of Bavaria.
> Albert, Duke of Saxony.
> Otto, Duke of Bavaria.
> Henry, Duke of Brunswick.
> Frederick, Count Palatine of Bavaria.
> Christopher, Duke of Bavaria.
> Eric, Duke of Brunswick.
> William, Duke of Juliers.
> Frederick, Margrave of Brandenburg.
> William, Landgrave, second, of Hesse.
> Christopher, Margrave of Baden.
> Sigismund, Margrave of Brandenburg.
> Albert, Margrave of Brandenburg.
> Casimir, Margrave of Brandenburg.
> Rodolph, Prince of Anhalt.
> The Prince of Chimay.

All these princes are decorated with the crown of honour.

COUNTS.

Another horseman magnificently dressed, and decorated with
the crown of honour, carrying a tablet on which are written
these words, "The celebrated counts and lords."

[44] These princes and counts, barons and knights, who follow after, are
frequently named by the authors who have written of the reign of Maximilian,
and particularly by Fugger, who, in the work often cited, details the important
services which they have rendered to their master, one of the rewards of which,
doubtless, is their place in this Triumph.

Count Albert of Zorn.
Count Frederick of Zorn.
Count Eitel Frederick of Zorn.
Count Ulric of Werdenberg.
Count Henry of Fürstenberg.
The Counts of Nassau.
The Counts of Frangipan.

HERREN.[45]

The Lords of Polheim.
The Lord of Vay.
Everard, Lord of Aremberg.
Pfeffers.
James, Lord of Luxemburg.
John, Lord of Berghes.
Veyt, Lord of Wolkenstein.*
Heyg of Milin.
The Lords of Lanno.
Cornelius, Lord of Berges.
Francis de Montibus.
Thierry, Lord of Tschernahor.
Morsperg.
Lord Christopher Weytmulner.

All these counts and lords are decorated with the crown of honour.

KNIGHTS.

Another horseman in magnificent costume, and decorated with the crown of honour, carrying a tablet on which is written, " The honourable knights."

The knights mounted, in ranks of five, bearing each his banner with his name.

[45] Barons.
* This and the three following are found in the German list, but omitted in the French.—ED.

Rembert, Lord of Reichenberg.
Frederick, Lord of Capelle.
William, Lord of Pappenheim.
Josse, Lord of Lalain.
John, Lord of Teschitz.
Ewald, Lord of Lichstenstein.
Gallin of Berghes.
John, Lord of Salazar.
Syrich, Lord of Zebitz.
Melchior, Lord of Massmünster.
Lord Reinhard May.
George, Lord of Ebenstein.
Ulric, Lord of Ankenrent.
Philip of Friburg.
Josse, Lord of Prantner.
Louis de Vaudrey.
Sixte, Lord of Trautson.
James of Ems.
Francis Schenk.
Charles de Saveuse.
Henry, Lord of Hundbiss.
Alferat.
Falkenstein.
James Valera.
Truchsess Christopher of Stetten.
James, Lord of Halder.
Leonard, Lord of Vetter.

They are all decorated with the crown of honour.

SOLDIERS OF MERIT.

A foot-soldier decorated with the crown of honour, carrying a
tablet, on which are inscribed these words : " The soldiers
of merit."

U

PL. 119. (Two ranks of five arquebusiers.)

These soldiers march in ranks of five, bearing their lances, each distinguished by his name, written on his coat or on the streamer attached to the crown of honour, with which his head is decorated. Their names are as follows :—

> Martin Schwarz.
> Manng of Schaffhaussen.
> Jenusch (Janusch).[46]
> John Talsat, Spaniard.
> Peter of Winterthur.*
> Peter Plarer.
> John Wanner.
> Richard Vantos (Vantois), Englishman.
> Conrad Hechinger.
> Weidehart.
> Henry Öterle, of the confederated cantons.
> Rap of Cilley.
> George of Ulm.
> John Ebwein.
> Peter Rörl.
> James Müllner.
> Spagörl, drummer.
> Jeckel, fifer, with the large fife.

(Three ensigns, and by their sides two halberdiers. The three ensigns bear on their flags the arms of the Empire, Austria, and Burgundy.

> One rank of halberdiers.

PL. 120. Two ranks of lancers with long lances.

Above the first rank are marked the following names :—

> Linsel.
> Fleck, of the confederate cantons.
> Löfling.

---

[46] Probably *Janos*, Hungarian for John, and pronounced Janoche.
* This name is not found in the German list.—ED.

Peter Wunderlich.

John Schwarz.

Ergot.

Two ranks of arquebusiers.)

PL. 121. *Two ranks with sabres.*

They are all decorated with the crown of honour.

BARRICADE OF WAGONS.

Herr Hans Wulfesdorfer, commander of the train, mounted, decorated with the crown of honour and carrying his couplet, which has not yet been composed.

Next comes the train of wagons.

All the attendants are decorated with the crown of honour.

SAVAGES OF CALICUT.

PL. 122 to 124. A savage of Calicut, naked (having a girdle round his loins, mounted on an elephant), wearing the crown of honour on his head and carrying a tablet, on which is written, "These people are subjects of the thrones and houses mentioned above."

Following are the savages of Calicut.

A rank armed with targets and swords.

A rank armed with pikes.

Two ranks with English bows and arrows.

They are all naked, or dressed in the Indian or Moorish fashion, and decorated with the crown of honour.

THE HEAVY BAGGAGE OF THE ARMY.

Jerome von Heremberg, commander of the heavy baggage-train, mounted, and carrying his couplet, which is not yet written.

PL. 125   The heavy baggage of the army (attended by different
to 129.   kinds of attendants and domestics) marching without
           order, mounted and on foot, according to the usual
           custom, with baggage-trains; and they are all deco-
           rated with the crown of honour.

END OF THE TRIUMPH.

APPENDIX.

PL. 130. A king and a queen (possibly Philip, King of the
          Romans, and Joanna, his wife) on horseback, clad
          in their royal robes, with the sceptre in the hand.
          They are preceded and followed by six foot-guards
          armed with pikes.

PL. 131. A princess on horseback, magnificently clad, with a
          crown upon her head and holding a little whip in
          her hand. Her horse is led by the bridle by two
          gentlemen. Behind her are two ladies of the court,
          also on horseback, richly dressed, and followed by
          three halberdiers.

PL. 132. A horseman carrying a tablet destined for a couplet,
          and followed by two men of a foreign nation, each
          of whom leads a horse saddled and equipped.

PL. 133, Two ranks of five men, in the costumes of different
  134.   nations, each leading a horse saddled and equipped.

PL. 135. The forepart of a triumphal car, drawn by four horses
          galloping, and driven by a winged genius, who holds
          a laurel crown in his left hand.

OBSERVATIONS ON THE TRIUMPH.

In the reproduction of the "Triumph" it has been found con-
venient to reduce the size of the plates to three-fourths of that of
the original. This reduction affects equally all the lines and the
black and white spaces, so that, although the effect produced is
to some extent different, the general characteristics are preserved.
When the edition of 1796 was printed, the wood blocks, having
lain unused for more than 250 years, had become warped and
worm-eaten, so that most of the plates show imperfections resulting
from one or both of those causes.

Each design is composed of several blocks fastened together,
and the warping of many of them has separated the edges, so that
white lines appear across those prints ; and in some cases the blocks
have been so bent that the edges have, in the printing, nearly cut
through the paper. The unevenness of the surface has also had the
effect of giving a faint impression and an appearance of rottenness
to the print. These defects necessarily appear in all the copies
of this work printed in 1796, and are faithfully copied in this reproduction, which is taken from a large paper copy. When the
blocks were found, the spaces on the banners, scrolls, and tablets
intended to carry the inscriptions were uncut ; but as these large
black spaces, which were not intended by the designer to remain,
injured materially the effect of the printed engravings, they were
in many instances cut away. Why this was not done in every
case is not explained, and those plates where the blackness
remains are as much injured in effect as the others would have
been had it not been removed. Up to No. 57, all the black
spaces are cut out ; afterwards, this is only done sometimes. It
has been deemed advisable, in the reproduction, to leave in every
case these spaces blank.

The numbering of the plates in the 1796 edition was very
carelessly done, so that in many cases the same numbers were
repeated on different plates, and do not agree with the numbers

given in the preface. In this reproduction, the numbering is as far as possible corrected, the numbers of the 1796 edition being given, and the true numbers added in brackets. The plates 89 to 100, which represent the wars of the Emperor, are so entirely different from the series of the wars in the picture on vellum, and from the descriptions in the manuscripts, that the editor of 1796 does not profess to have found the correct order. He notices only No. 89, the Venetian War, which can be recognized from the winged lion. No. 94 was probably intended as the preface to the wars, as it has two large tablets for inscriptions; and No. 93 is certainly the Austrian War, as the Emperor appears accompanied by a crowned female figure carrying the Austrian flag, and the arms also appear on the car: in addition to this there is a figure which seems intended to represent a navigable river, probably the Danube.

From No. 105 to 129, the original numbering of the plates is altogether incorrect. The arrangement of those numbered 110, 111, 125, 129, and 128 only needs special mention. Jackson* has fallen into an error in placing these plates, as he says of them: "It is evident that some are wanting, for the two which may be considered as the first and last of those five respectively require a preceding and a following cut to render them complete; and there are also one or two cuts wanting to complete the intermediate subjects." He places them in the following order,— 129, 128, 110, 111, 125.

By placing them in the order in which they appear in the reproduction, they form a consecutive series, but are short of a cut before 110 (125), which should contain the horses for the waggon in that plate. Passavant describes the missing print, which is contained in the ancient copy in the Imperial library at Vienna. It contains Jerom von Heremberg, as commander of the baggage, holding his tablet. Passavant,† in giving the order in which these cuts should appear, has overlooked the general arrangement, by which the head of the procession appears as No. 1, and has reversed the true order. He alters 128 to 125, and places Jerom von Heremberg as No. 129*, following his new number 129. The copy of the "Triumph" which he has used has been, apparently, numbered differently to that seen by Jackson and that used for

---

* "A Treatise on Wood Engraving," by Jackson and Chatto, p. 301.
† "Peintre-Graveur," vol. iii. p. 269.

the reproduction, since he refers to Nos. 110 and 111 as 126
and 127.

The arrangement adopted in the reproduction is as follows :--

> No. (125), in 1796 edition No. 110.
> No. (126),　　　,,　　　No. 111.
> No. (127),　.　,,　　　No. 125.
> No. (128),　　　,,　　　No. 129.
> No. (129),　.　,,　　　No. 128.

Passavant also notices another engraving found in the Vienna
library, and for which the wood block has been lost, representing
the triumphal car of Philip I. and Joanna of Castile. This was
intended to follow No. 135, which contains the four horses driven
by a winged figure, the two forming one design.

In comparing the engravings with the description prepared by
the order of the Emperor for the instruction of the designer, it
will be found that there are others besides those already mentioned
in which the instructions have not been followed. The Car of
Natural Fools, Plate 30, contains only five instead of six fools.
The Soldiers, Plate 119, have not their names written on the
dress, but scrolls are placed above the procession for that purpose, and the Savages of Calicut, Nos. 122 to 124, are treated
in a more picturesque manner than the Emperor intended.

The editor of the descriptions in 1796 omitted to insert reference numbers to Plates 41, Hans von Yfan, and 42, a rank of
five men on foot. Although he is open to censure for the care-
lessness displayed in matters of this kind, yet he does not deserve
the sweeping condemnation which Jackson* pronounces against
him. The preface gives all the information then obtainable with
regard to the history of the work, to which more modern research
has added little. The notes, explanatory of the cuts and of the
difficulties which are met with in the manuscript descriptions, are
in most cases valuable aids to an understanding of the subjects,
but there are some few errors and omissions which may be noticed
here.

Plate 6. One of the falconers carries an owl. This bird was
used in falconry as a siren to attract the kite, so as to enable the
hawk to approach it more easily.

---

* Jackson and Chatto, pp. 289 and 292.

"On se sert du duc dans la fauconnerie pour attirer le milan ; on attache au duc une queue de renard, pour rendre sa figure encore plus extraordinaire ; il vole à fleur de terre, et se pose dans la campagne, sans se percher sur aucun arbre ; le milan, qui l'aperçoit de loin, arrive et s'approche du duc, non pas pour le combattre ou l'attaquer, mais comme pour l'admirer, et il se tient auprès de lui assez long tems, pour se laisser tirer par le chasseur, ou prendre par les oiseaux de proie qu'on lâche à sa poursuite."—"Histoire Naturelle des Oiseaux," par de Buffon, par Sonnini, tom. iv. p. 40.

Plate 18, Note 7. In this note it is erroneously stated that the rebec is our present violincello, as may be seen in the woodcut, and it is added, it is tuned in fifths. This is hardly correct, though the tuning in both instruments is the same : the instrument as given in the engraving has seven strings. It would be more correctly described as the viol de gamba, or leg viol, an old musical instrument with six strings, so called because it was held between the legs. It was derived from the rebec, a Moorish instrument with two strings, to which the Spaniards added a third. This number was afterwards increased to six. This instrument has been used in modern orchestras on rare occasions.

Plate 26, Note 13. The Bishop of Vienna is the only ecclesiastic who appears in the procession, and he only appears as kapellmeister, and not in his sacerdotal character. This is the more remarkable, as Maximilian professed to be the head of Christendom, and desired at one time to be made Pope himself.

Plate 42, Note 18. The history of armour is now better understood, and descriptions and illustrations of the various kinds of helmets will be found in "Weapons of War," by Auguste Demmin, translated by C. C. Black, M.A. London, Bell & Daldy. 1870.

Plate 55 is described as the Course à la queue. The German is Schweifrennen, which might be translated into English as the train or tail course.

Plate 56, Note 37. This note does not throw much light on the meaning of the name given to this course. The wreath is said to have been introduced into Europe by the Crusaders, who copied it from the Saracens, and was worn over the helmet below the crest. In English heraldry, its colours are derived from the coat-of-arms, in later times; but on its first introduction, there would be no such rule observed.

The wreaths in the engraving are worn upon a cap of leather or cloth, and it is doubtless called the course of the wreath from the wreath being the principal protection to the head, and not a mere adjunct to the helmet.

Plate 82. The reference to this plate is wrongly given, as there are only the first three provinces represented out of the six named. It is evident that there is a wood block for the last three missing.

Besides this there are many other breaks in the series of designs, which are the result either of the blocks not having been found, or possibly of their not having been engraved. This latter is, as regards the greater number of omissions, the more probable, as there are no breaks before the 36th block. Following the Plate No. 36, a cut representing five men with battleaxes is missing; following No. 51, the Elmet Course; following No. 53, the Course of Gaspar Wintzer and the Vamplate Course; following No. 56, the Marriage of Burgundy; following No. 82, the standards of Artois, Holland, and Zeland; following No. 88, the Marriage of the Emperor; following No. 102, the Hungarian Trophy Car. Before Plate 103 there is a plate of Horsemen carrying Standards, missing; and following both the Nos. 103, 118, and the intervening plates, there are many missing blocks. Between Nos. 119, 120, and 121 there are several blocks missing; and following No. 121, the Barricade of Wagons; following No. 124, Jerom von Heremberg; and following No. 135, the Triumphal Car of Philip and his wife.

At the back of many of the wood blocks the names of the engravers are written in ink, and in the preface to the "Triumph," which is followed by Bartsch, these are stated to be :—

1. Jerome Andre.
2. Jean de Bonn.
3. Cornelius.
4. Hans Frank.
5. Saint German.
6. Guillaume.
7. Corneille Liefrink.
8. Guillaume Liefrink.

9. Alexis Lindt.
10. Josse de Negker.
11. Vincent Pfarkecher.
12. Jaques Rupp.
13. Hans Schaufelein.
14. Jean Taberith.
15. F P.
16. H F in a monogram.
17. W R.

The present keeper of the Imperial library, Herr Anton Ritter von Perger, has kindly furnished, in a letter to the editor of this reproduction, the following as the correct list, and has added the number of blocks executed by each :—

Hans Schaufelein...	...	...	1	block.
Jerom Andre	...	...	5	,,
... Schriftler	...	...	16	,,
Hans Taberith	...	...	13	,,
Wilhelm Lieferink		...	14	,,
Cornelis Lieferink		...	4	,,
Hans Lieferink	...	...	1	,,
Jobst Danneck	...	...	10	,,
Jan de Bon	...	...	9	,,
Cornelis May	...	...	5	,,
Hans Frank	...	...	2	,,
Alexis Lindt	...	...	2	,,
Jacob Rupp	...	...	2	,,
W R	...	...	2	,,
HF (Hans Frank?) ...		...	6	,,
N ...	...	...	1	,,

The two lists do not agree entirely, as the first contains Cornelius, Saint German, Guillaume, Vincent Pfarkecher, and the initials F P, not contained in the latter; and that contains Schriftler, Hans Lieferink, Cornelis May, and the initial N, which are not found in the former. It is singular that there should have been any mistake about these names, as the editor of the "Triumph" and Bartsch, who was the keeper of the Royal Library, had access to the blocks themselves. It may be remarked, however, that the Cornelius of one list is probably the

Cornelis May or Cornelis Lieferink of the other, and Guillaume is no doubt Wilhelm Lieferink; but the others cannot be identified.

Besides these names, written on the back of the blocks, there are marks on the plates, some of which may be those of engrave.s. The first "Wisend," however, evidently refers to the bison in the design, and some of the others appear to be numerals. These marks are as follows :—

On Plate 25	...	...	...	**.WISEND .**
,, 58	...	...	...	
,, 64	...	...	...	
,, 67	...	...	...	
,, 68	...	...	...	
,, 69	...	...	...	
,, 71	...	...	...	
,, 72	...	...	...	
,, 73	...	...	...	
,, 80 (81)	...	...	...	
,, 83 (84)	...	...	...	
,, 86 (87)	...	...	...	

Burgmair's mark, H B, appears upon many of the plates, but the majority have no mark of any kind, and the unequal merit of the design and the drawing has led Jackson, in his " Treatise on Wood Engraving," to doubt whether they were all the work of Burgmair himself. He says (p. 293) : " At the back of the block which corresponds with the description numbered 120, Hans Schaufflein's name is found coupled with that of Cornelius Lie-frink; and at the back of the cut which corresponds with the description numbered 121 Schaufflein's name occurs alone. The occurrence of Schaufflein's name at the back of the cuts would certainly seem to indicate that he was one of the engravers; but his name also appearing at the back of that described under No. 120, in conjunction with the name of Cornelius Liefrink, who was certainly a wood-engraver, makes me inclined to sup-pose that he might only have made the drawing on the block, and not have engraved the cut; and this supposition seems to be partly confirmed by the fact that the cuts which are numbered 104, 105, and 106, corresponding with the descriptions Nos. 119, 120, and 121, have not Hans Burgmair's mark, and are much more like the undoubted designs of Hans Schaufflein than those of that artist. That the cuts published under the title of the ' Triumphs of Maximilian' were not all drawn on the block by the same person will, I think, appear probable to any one who even cursorily examines them; and whoever carefully compares them can scarcely have a doubt on the subject." He then draws attention to the spirited design of the drawings incontestably Burgmair's, to the strength and heaviness of the horses, the muscular form of the men, and the natural action and the drawing of the hoofs of the horses, mentioning particularly Nos. 15, 27, and 33. With these he contrasts the series of banner-bearers, Nos. 57 to 88, which he says are "remarkable for laboured and stiff drawing, gaunt and meagre men, and leggy starved-like cattle." He objects to the action of the horses and the drawing of the hoofs. He proceeds: "Not only are the men and horses represented according to a different standard, but even the very ground is indicated in a different manner."

There certainly is a great difference between the designs alluded to; but even among those which bear Burgmair's mark there are some much inferior to others, and the hoofs of the horses are not in all cases well drawn. It is possible also that Burgmair's son should have assisted in the designs—a not improbable supposition, and one which would account for the inferiority which certainly exists. From Dienecker's letter, quoted in the notice of the life of Burgmair, it would seem as if he sometimes transferred the design to the wood; and if he was accustomed to do so, others might be employed in the same way. Dienecker himself would no doubt have been able to copy with fidelity, but others of less sureness of hand might travesty the design in drawing on the wood. Burgmair may therefore have made the designs of the banner-bearers, which may have been transferred to the wood by an inferior draughtsman. This is the more probable, as Burgmair drew animals with great truth and power, and evinced a thorough knowledge of their habits and character, as may be seen in all the earlier designs of the series of the Triumph; and he drew the human figure equally well. If his design was transferred to the wood by one who had studied only to draw the human figure, and who had no knowledge of the construction and movements of the horse, the result would probably be similar to what we find in the series of the banner-bearers. The men would be drawn much better than the horses. Against this theory must be put the fact that some of the horses exhibit a want of harmony in the action of the legs which must have existed in the original design, a want of harmony similar to that found in Schaufelein's early work, as is seen in the illustrations to Sir Theurdank. Jackson formed too low an opinion of Schaufelein, not apparently knowing his best work, the "Marriage Dance," which is of extreme rarity. Ottley, in his "Inquiry," vol. ii. p. 756, expresses the opinion that Schaufelein may have made a few of the designs of the "Triumph." There are seventeen cuts, Nos. 89 to 103, which present some difficulties also, and Jackson confidently states (page 290) that sixteen of them, 89 to 99 and 101 to 103, are not by Burgmair. He omits No. 100, which is precisely similar in drawing to the other sixteen; but he was no doubt induced to do this because the four horses in that plate are the same group as those in No. 135, which is undoubtedly by Burgmair. These again may have been designed by Burgmair, but not drawn on the wood by him.

Jackson admits the possibility of this supposition, although he leans strongly to the opinion that there were more designers than one.

The plates Nos. 125 to 129 are a source of as much difficulty as any, since they only have a background, and they are very differently drawn from any of the others. Jackson inclines to attribute them to Durer, but without giving any sufficient reason; but Mr. W. B. Scott, who has given considerable study to Durer's works, pronounces a very decided opinion to the contrary.

Mr. Scott's reasons for coming to this conclusion, and Dr. Willshire's for holding an opposite opinion, are printed from letters (to be found at the end of this division) kindly sent by those gentlemen to the editor.

From Mr. Scott's letter it will be seen that he leans strongly to the opinion that Burgmair designed the whole series; and from Dr. Willshire's, that he favours the opinion of Jackson, that several designers were employed. These letters are printed *in extenso*, as valuable contributions towards the solution of an obscure problem.

The whole of the series of the "Triumph" is not uniform in the scale of the designs and the height and size of the figures. Even among those bearing Burgmair's mark the difference is very great. The whole series may be divided into several series, each series differing in these respects from the other, but the plates in each agreeing together.

The cutting of the blocks follows a similar division, and is not of uniform merit. Jackson, whose opinions are upon this point of the greatest value, as he was a practical wood-engraver of considerable ability and knowledge, says (p. 304): "The best engraved cuts are to be found among those which contain Burgmair's mark. Some of the banner-bearers are also very ably executed, though not in so free or bold a manner; which I conceive to be owing to the more laboured style in which the subject has been drawn on the block. The mechanical subjects, with their accompanying figures, are the worst engraved as well as the worst drawn of the whole. The fine cuts which I suppose to have been designed by Albert Durer are engraved with great spirit, but not so well as the best of those which contain the mark of Burgmair." Jackson does not seem to have remarked the difference in the style of cutting of some of the later pieces bearing Burgmair's mark, such as the Savages of Calicut, Nos. (122) and (123), from the earlier. Thus there are four or five hands only apparent in the cutting, although there were at least sixteen engravers employed upon the work. This result was gained, there can be no doubt, by the pieces which have similar characteristics having been finished by the same engraver. As the work was in progress during four years, from 1516 to 1519, when the Emperor died, there would be ample time for one engraver to finish the cutting of many blocks, if they had been carried to some degree of completeness when put into his hands. This course had already been pursued in the earlier works for the Emperor, as we learn from the letter of Dienecker, already alluded to, and which is given in Herberger's "Conrad Peutinger in his Relations with the Emperor Maximilian I."*

He writes on the 20th of October, 1512 :—

"I have been told that your Imperial majesty wishes that the work and piece-work which I prepare and do should be rather pushed on, &c., and that you have written to Doctor Bewtinger on that account to give me the assistance of two or three more form-cutters. I am very glad of it, your majesty, and as 1 know two form-cutters who are very clever, and would like to be employed by me in your majesty's service, . . . I should be glad if your majesty would give orders that the two form-cutters may enter my service ; and let each of them be accredited to Bamgartner for a hundred florins a year, in order that I may retain them with me and they may have enough to live.

"Under these circumstances I shall be ready to prepare all work for the cutters, and will afterwards finish and polish † it with my own hands, in order that the work and piece-work should be all alike in the cut, and finished all by the same hand, so that nobody could doubt it.

"Being then three workers instead of myself alone, I pledge myself to furnish your majesty six or seven good pieces a month, all done in my very best style; and after my wish has been granted, Schonsperger may begin to print. I shall do my very best, and exercise my best skill to push the work and please your majesty.

"May it likewise please your majesty to give orders that we three cutters may have a private room or house, that we may be alone and unmolested, as the work requires it that we should be."

The "Triumph" was never completed, being, like all the art-works of Maximilian, interrupted by his death, and not resumed by his successor. The wood blocks were laid aside, and after a

---

* "Conrad Peutinger in seinem Verhaltnisse zum Kaiser Maximilian I." Theodor Herberger. Augsburg, 1851, p. 29, note 91.

† The wood blocks, when the engraving is completed, are polished by being rubbed with the hand.

time lost sight of and believed to be destroyed, until their discovery at the end of the last century. A few impressions had,
according to Bartsch,* been taken as proofs in a slovenly manner
from some of them upon odd pieces of paper. M. Mariette
possessed 87, and the king of Sweden a like number, as is stated
in the catalogue of M. Mariette's collection, 1775. Sandrart had
seen a hundred. The Imperial Court library possesses an ancient
copy, formerly in the library of the Archduke Ferdinand, which
contains, according to the present keeper, in his letter to the
editor, which has been mentioned earlier, 135 plates; Bartsch
says 90, and Passavant, 128. The difference is easily explainable,
on the supposition that the collection has been added to.

There is another copy in that library, which was printed in 1796
on parchment, and another on paper, of the same date, which
latter contains only 127 plates.

The editor has been favoured by Mr. Reid, the keeper of the
print-room of the British Museum, with an account of the prints
of the " Triumph " which it contains. Among them is a volume
of early proofs, which was originally in the Ottley collection, afterwards passed into that of Mr. Coningham, and was acquired by
the Museum in 1845. If Bartsch's description of the greatest
part of the early impressions known in his time is correct, the
Museum is especially fortunate in possessing this series of early
impressions, which are generally fine.

It contains impressions from two of the lost blocks,—Jerome
von Heremberg, and the Triumphal Car drawn by the horses, in
Plate 135. Passavant mentions (No. 81) similar impressions
from these two blocks as existing in the Imperial library at
Vienna, and describes the watermark on both the sheets on
which they are printed as "un écusson en cœur avec une fau-
cille." The watermark of the paper of the series in the British
Museum, a facsimile of which is given on next page, is a double
eagle ensigned and charged with a sickle. It is most probable that
Passavant intended to describe the same watermark, and if that
is so, the impressions were probably struck off at the same time.

Besides the Ottley series, the Museum possesses three early
proofs which were in the old Museum collection, and are believed
to have originally formed part of the Cracherode collection. They
correspond in subject with Nos. 44, 76, and 110 of the edition of
1796. The last, of which the subject is, " Captives surrounded

* Vol. vii. p. 235.

by a chain," is a remarkably fine impression, and contrasts very favourably with even large paper copies of the 1796 edition, although the block does not seem to have suffered by age so much as some of the others.

The trustees of the British Museum have permitted the HOL-BEIN SOCIETY to photograph the two unpublished plates for the purpose of reproducing them. They are reproduced uniformly

Y

with the others, on a scale of three-fourths of the size of the originals. As far as is known, there are only two impressions, those above mentioned, and as they have never been before copied, they must be considered to add considerable interest to this publication of the HOLBEIN SOCIETY.

Jerome von Heremberg is numbered in the Museum list 124*, but in this reproduction 124^A. It contains Jerome von Heremberg on horseback, followed by country people also on horseback, and two horses driven by a peasant carrying a large whip over his shoulder. These horses draw the waggon in Plate 110 (125), and there is part of a tree at the side, which completes the tree in that design.

The other plate is numbered 102** in the Museum list, but in this reproduction 135^A. It follows the team of four horses driven by a genius, No. 135. It is singular that a man is introduced assisting to turn one of the wheels.

Dr. Willshire has drawn the attention of the editor to a notice of the "Triumph" in Retberg's "Dürer's Kupperstiche v. Holzschnitte, &c.," Munich, 1871, in which it is stated that Dr. M. Thausing, president of the Albertina, discovered, by a careful comparison of the sketches in the Ambras and Albertina collections, and of the plates in the Triumphal Arch and Triumphal Car, and from an allusion of Neudorffer's, that the designs of twenty-four of the plates are by Albert Durer, and he gives as his, Plates 89 to 103, 104 to 108, 130, 131, and 135.

At present it is impossible to determine the value of the results which he has arrived at, as the evidence upon which the conclusion is formed is not accessible ; but among the designs said to be by Durer are some of the worst in the procession.

Letters from Mr. SCOTT *and* Dr. WILLSHIRE.

From WILLIAM B. SCOTT, Esq., Author of "Half-hour Lectures
on the History and Practice of the Fine and Ornamental
Arts"; "Albert Durer: his Life and Works," &c. Long-
mans, Green, & Co. 1869.

" On receiving your note I have again looked at the Burgkmairs,
and considered over again your reasons for supposing it likely
that Durer * assisted that artist in some of the 'Triumphs of Maximilian.' I am still, however, of the same opinion, and fancy that
if we were together, with the prints before us, you would consider
my reasons good for retaining the conviction that the Nuremberg
artist did not assist, or at least that he did not actually do any
of the sheets of the procession, nor any complete figures of the
extensive work of the Augsburger. The speculation is, however,
an interesting one, and worth considering in your literary accompaniment to the volume of the HOLBEIN SOCIETY's reprint. The
reason you assign in proof of Durer having put his hand to the
work,—that other designs in the 'Triumph' are occasionally so
very inferior that he must have received help, where the drawing
is so good,—is only a negative one. Burgkmair was nearly always
a careless draughtsman, with a wild freedom, both in the use of
the instrument wherewith he drew on the block and in the action
of his figures. The expression of his faces, too, has always an
emphatic peculiarity. Durer's manner, on the contrary, had an
extraordinary amenity, his grotesque was premeditated, and his
faces are all thinking rather than acting faces. The difference
between the two would have been apparent, and left no doubt
on the observer's mind. Some other able artist might be found
perhaps who had the faculty, and did not mind exercising it, of
imitating, while assisting, the long labour of Burgkmair. Hans
Sebald Beham, for example, in his large print of the 'Pillaging

---

* The opinion of the editor upon this subject has been modified since he
wrote the letter to which Mr. Scott refers, as will be seen in the preceding
pages.

Train,' on four great blocks, shows much the same vigour as Burgkmair; but Durer, throughout the ' Triumphal Arch,' an immense undertaking, enough to try his patience, never loses his careful handling and refined touch.   But it appears to me Burgk- mair needed no aid; he was unboundedly prolific, only he seems to have made no preliminary sketch, and to have left the drawing on the block as good or bad luck would have it.   He is therefore a very unequal artist, although always, or nearly always, a man of startling power and invention.   If his worst things are bad, his best are extraordinarily fine.   ' Death and the Lovers,' one of the rarest early German chiaroscuro prints, of which I could show you a very fine impression, is in the highest degree splendid.   So is the ' St. Luke painting the Virgin,' a woodcut not very large, wherein the pose of the Madonna and the faces of the two principal figures are so sweet and refined, they are equal to any Italian work of the period, combined with individuality and appropriateness belonging to his own German nature."

Mr. Scott, carrying out his views, has omitted from his ex- haustive catalogue of Dürer's works the six cuts in the " Triumph."

———

Extract from a letter from WILLIAM HUGHES WILLSHIRE, Esq., M.D. Edin., late President of the Medical Society of London, &c.; author of " An Introduction to the Study and Collection of Ancient Prints."   Ellis & White, London, 1874.

" In reply to your questions of the 20th ult., I may say that I had always considered Chatto's critical exposition ('Treatise on Wood Engraving,' by Jackson & Chatto, 2nd edition, pp. 289 et seq.) of the cuts of the Triumphal Procession as true an one as it was possible to give of a matter much of which, after all, must remain a question of opinion, and can never become of demon- strative certainty.   Since I heard from you I have again gone over the two copies of the Triumphal Procession in the British Museum, with Chatto's critique in hand, and the result is that I am of the same opinion still.   That Burgkmair was the designer of the majority of the cuts in question not any one can dispute, of course.   There is documentary evidence that he was engaged on the work; many cuts bear both his initial marks and characteristic style, and others evince the style, though the marks are absent. But with this allowance, I think it should be admitted that there are perhaps nearly fifty cuts which neither bear Burgkmair's mark nor evince his style. On the contrary, in many of these not only is the style not Burgkmair's—negatively, as it were,—but it is positively somebody else's, so individual and marked is it. In illustration of this, I would refer to what Chatto says respecting the joints and the hoofs of the horses and the general forms of the latter, of the treatment of the ground in cuts 57 to 88, and of the peculiar style of some of the subsequent cuts of the series, in which the pine-trees play a prominent part. These cuts from 57 to 103, with the after ones (which evince a Düreresque feeling), show neither the H B nor Burgkmair's power, *quoad* 57 to 103, nor his style, *quoad* the remainder. Who were the designers of these doubtful pieces then? All that can be said for certain is, that H. Schäufelin's name is on the back of one of the blocks, of which block he was probably cutter as well as designer, and hence his name on it without that of anybody else; while on another block his name occurs with that of Liefrink, who probably engraved in part Schäufelin's design. Schäufelin was not accustomed to cut his own designs, as shown by the letter of Dienecker, in which, says Passavant, ' Dienecker se plaint que la dessinateur ou peintre, Hans Schäufelin, n'ait pas encore été payée pour les dessins qu'il lui a livrés, et prie S. M. de vouloir bien en remettre le montant,' &c. Further, if Dürer was engaged, as we know he was, to design part of the great works the Arch and the Car, why may he not have contributed those latter cuts of the series of the procession, which are not Burgkmair's, are too good for Schäufelin, and are really like the style of Dürer?

"The same may be said of the Weiss Kunig as of the Triumphal Procession. I think that, though Burgkmair was the designer of most of the cuts, he certainly was not of the whole; as on 200 is Schäufelin's mark, on 199 Springenklee's, and on 78 **₺B** I question if 33, 34, and 35 are H B's, or 41, 47, 95, 150, 236, &c.

APPENDIX.

APPENDIX.

————o————

VEHME-GERICHTE.

DURING the reign of Maximilian the Vehm-Gerichte* was becoming the subject of general discussion and public opposition; the Institution, which in earlier times was only mentioned in awe-struck whispers, was now openly denounced, and its mysteries made public property, by the hand of Æneas Silvius (Pius II.). In its prevailing days death was the penalty for divulging the names of the promoters or the proceedings of their tribunals, and the utmost secrecy was secured. The date of their establishment is as little known as the origin of the name. Leibnitz suggests Fehm, as derived from the Latin *fama*, common report, and *geright*, tribunal; but we need scarcely go further than the archaic German word *feme*, condemnation, which gives us at once a criminal court. They bore another name, the Carolinian Courts, from their supposed institution by Charlemagne. The first clear evidence of their existence is in the year 1267, when a document was issued from one of these courts under the presidency of Bernard of Henedorp, freeing one Gervin of Kinkenrode from feudal service for his inheritance of Broke, for lands held under the Count of Mark.

The jurisdiction of these courts extended over the whole of ancient Westphalia, embracing the lands between the Weser and the Rhine. The lawlessness and anarchy of the Middle Ages, when might ever prevailed over right, necessitated the establishment of courts which paid little respect to rank, and had power enough to execute their judgments with speed and secrecy.

---

* Dr. Berck, in his work, "Geschichte der Westphälischen Femgerichte," Bremen, 1815 ("The History of the Westphalian Vehm Gerichte"), collected all available information on this subject. See "Secret Societies of the Middle Ages." Nattali. London, 1848.

Z

The supreme power and authority of the Vehme may be understood by the fact that no writer dares so much as mention their
name till the middle of the fourteenth century, when Henry of
Hervorden, a Dominican monk, wrote against them; and a
century later, when Æneas Silvius (Pius II.), then Frederick's
secretary, computed the number of the initiated at 100,000; and
no instance had been known of a single person divulging their
secrets.

Although secret, so far from being illegal courts, they reckoned
amongst the initiated the highest nobles, and sometimes the
Emperors, either personally or by deputy. Each tribunal lord
had his separate district, and either sat himself or appointed a
Free count as deputy. When he presented his deputy, he took
oath that the count was born on Westphalian soil, that his father
and mother were so born, that he had committed no crime and
was of good repute. The income of the Free count was considerable, and was derived from fines and presents from the free
Schöppen, or initiated, and also from a fixed allowance in money
or in kind. Next to the count were the Schöppen, or assessors.
They formed the main body of the society. A solemn ceremony
attended the initiation of a candidate. Kneeling, with his hand
upon a sword and halter, he took the following oath :—

"I promise on the holy marriage, that I will from henceforth
aid, keep, and conceal the holy Fehms from wife and child, from
father and mother, from sister and brother, from fire and wind,
from all that the sun shines upon and the rain covers, from all
that is between sky and ground, especially from the man who
knows the law, and will bring before this free tribunal under which
I sit, all that belongs to the secret jurisdiction of the Emperor,
whether I know it to be true myself or have heard it from trustworthy people, whatever requires correction or punishment, whatever is Fehm-free [a crime committed in the county], that it may
be judged, or, with the consent of the accuser, be put off in grace;
and will not cease to do so for love or for fear, for gold or for
silver, or for precious stones, and will strengthen this tribunal and
jurisdiction with all my five senses and power; and that I do not
take upon me this office for any other cause than for the sake of
right and justice; moreover, that I will ever further and honour
this free tribunal more than any other free tribunals; and what I
thus promise will I steadfastly and firmly keep, so held me God
and his Holy Gospel."

After this he swore that he would ever, to the best of his ability, enlarge the holy empire, and that he would undertake nothing with unrighteous hand against the land and people of the Stuhlherr (tribunal lord).

The Schöppe, after this, was initiated, the mysteries of the tribunal were revealed, and the secret sign was communicated. He was further informed of the dreadful death which awaited him if he forgot his vow. In such a case he was blindfolded, his tongue was pulled out, and he was hung seven feet higher than any other felon.

For the lawful holding of a Vehm court other officers were necessary; Frohnbotten (holy messengers or servants of God), who acted as sergeants or messengers, and a clerk to enter the decisions in the *Blood-book*.

Amongst the initiated were persons of various ranks, from the highest to the lowest freeman, so that every man might be tried by his peers.

The authority of the Emperor alone was recognized as controlling the decrees of the court.

The Count held two kinds of courts—one open, one secret. The open court was held three times a year at least, and at this every householder in the county was bound, under a penalty, to appear and to declare an oath what crimes he knew to have been committed in the county. The secret courts were held in the open air, and in daylight, and instant death was the penalty of intrusion by the uninitiated. Persons caught in the actual commission of crimes, whether noble or not, were executed on the spot; if they escaped, they were cited to appear and tried in due form.

The Emperors found this tribunal of such value to them that they extended its jurisdiction over the whole empire.

The court had power, in case of contumacy or non-appearance after citation, to order a sentence of outlawry, and from that day the offender was liable, when caught, to be hanged on the nearest tree with a withy branch; a knife was stuck by his side, to show that he had not been murdered. The court had power to sentence princes and towns to outlawry, with the immediate loss of all privileges. If the citation was attended to, due regard to justice was observed, and an appeal, in case of condemnation, allowed to the Imperial Chamber at Dortmund, or to the Emperor or king. If the Emperor was initiated, he heard the cause himself; if not initiated, he referred it to such of his counsellors as were. In the fifteenth century several princes were cited to appear, and Duke Henry of Bavaria was obliged to become a free-schöppe to save himself.

Maximilian's father, Frederick, at last fell under the ban of the tribunal, and he was cited in 1470, with his chancellor, to appear between the gates of Wunnenberg to defend his person and highest honour, under penalty of being held a disobedient emperor. He treated the citation with contempt.

Maximilian, on his accession, superseded the authority of the Vehm tribunal by that of the Imperial Chamber, and by dividing the empire into circles, each with its tribunals of justice. He outlawed the Duke of Wurtemberg, whom the tribunal would have justified. This institution was never wholly and formally abolished, but lingered on with diminished powers. In some districts they were abolished by special decree, and where they claimed jurisdiction, exemptions and privileges against them were multiplied; they were denounced by different diets, held their courts in absolute secrecy, and, hunted down by an enraged population, gradually died out.

Undoubtedly these courts had become utterly corrupt and venial, but still it was a bold thing for Maximilian to strike at their very existence, as their early protective value to the weak, the certainty and celerity of the punishment of offenders, had on the one side endeared them to the peasants, and created a feeling of perhaps ill-defined awe amongst the higher ranks of the community.

MAXIMILIAN AND HIS DAUGHTER MARGARET.

AFTER the battle of Liege, won by Maximilian, the ambassadors of the Emperor and of Louis XI. met at Arras, the principal city of Artois, and after long deliberation it was considered that the marriage of Margaret to the dauphin would best secure oblivion of their mutual wrongs. This was decided on, and it was arranged that the young girl should be sent to

France. Throughout the kingdom, on her progress to Paris, Margaret was received by applauding crowds as the mediator of peace. She was sent for from Amboise, whither Louis had ordered the members of his family and other noble persons to meet together. On arriving at Paris, the king confirmed the marriage publicly, and the betrothal and rites having been celebrated, the day was spent as a public holiday.

What Gerard Roo speaks of as a betrothal, Commines speaks of as a marriage; further, Dupont (vol. iii. p. 352 *et seq.*) writes thus: Margaret was then three years and a half old, and the dauphin rather more than twelve. Their meeting took place on Sunday, the 22nd of June, 1483, at a place called Metairie le Rayne, near Amboise. "The dauphin," says a contemporary letter, "left the castle of Amboise dressed in a robe of crimson satin, lined with black velvet, and mounted on a hackney, and attended with thirty archers. At the bridge he dismounted, after having saluted the ladies and changed his dress, and put on a long robe of cloth of gold. Presently the dauphiness arrived and descended from her litter, and immediately they were betrothed by the prothonotary, nephew of the Grand Seneschal of Normandy, who demanded of the dauphin in a loud voice, so that all could hear him, if he would have Margaret of Austria in marriage? and he answered, 'Yes'; and the complemental question was put to the dauphiness, who gave the same answer. Upon which they joined hands, and the dauphin kissed the dauphiness twice; and they then returned to their lodgings. And the streets of Amboise were hung with cloth, and in the market-place was a figure of a siren, who spouted forth white wine and red from her breasts." The next day, the ceremony of marriage took place in the chapel of the castle.

In strange contrast with her gallant reception by the dauphin was his ignominious dismissal and repudiation of her when she had attained her thirteenth year.

This curious woodcut, produced below, and bearing on the subject, of which M. T. Ph. Berjeau has obligingly sent me a stereotype, appeared in his publication the "Bibliophile."* Dr. Willshire drew my attention to it, and copied the passage in the publication for me, which, as he says, is "out of print and extremely difficult to procure."

---

* "Le Bibliophile," tome ii. p. 68. Paris, June, 1863.

"Lorsqu'elle [*i. e.* Anne de Bretagne] devint en suite la femme de Charles VIII., malgrè son précédent mariage avec Maximilien, celui-ci fut naturellement furieux de la double injure

qui lui faisait subir cette union. Tous les Allemands ressentirent comme lui cette injure, et c'est ce qui fut l'occasion d'un échange assez amer d'épîtres en vers et en prose entre Jacques Wimpheling de Schlestadt, qui habitait Spire en 1492, et Robert Gaguin, général de Trinitaires, que ses travaux avaient amené à Heidelberg dans la même année. Leurs lettres furent publiées peu de temps après en un petit volume, in-4to de 12 ff., sans lieu ni date, mais probablement imprimé à Strasbourg, sous ce titre, ' Disceptatio oratorū duorum regū / Romani, scilicet et Franci, super ra/ptū Illustrissime ducisse britannice.' Au-dessous du titre est le petit bois gravé, que nous reproduisons ici, et qui représente sans doute Marguerite d'Autriche venant rendre à son père son contrat de mariage brisé par Charles YIII. On se demande pourquoi l'artiste a couronné le père et la fille d'une auréole, car ni l'un ni l'autre n'ont été canonisés après leur mort, et ne pouvaient l'être d'ailleurs de leur vivant. La seule explication possible est peut-être que l'artiste a voulu flatter ainsi la prétention étrange de Maximilien, qui se faisait appeler Pontifex Maximus, à l'exemple des empereurs romains, et voulait absolument que le Pape le prît comme coadjuteur dans le pontificat romain."— (" Le Bibliophile illustré," vol. ii. p. 68.)

TRANSLATION.

"When she (*i. e.* Anne of Brittany) became the wife of Charles VIII., notwithstanding her previous marriage with Maximilian, he was naturally enraged by the double outrage to which he was subjected by this union. All the Germans, in common with him, resented this wrong, and thus sprung the occasion of an exchange of bitter letters, both in verse and prose, between James Wimpheling of Schlestadt, who lived at Spire in 1492, and Robert Gaguin, general of the order of the Trinity,* whose duties had brought him to Heidelberg in the same year. Their letters were published a short time after in a small quarto volume of twelve leaves, without place or date, probably printed at Strasbourg, under the title, ' Disceptatio oratorū duorum regū Romani, scilicet et Franci, super raptū Illustrissime ducisse britannice.' Below the title is the little wood-engraving, which we reproduce here, and which represents without doubt Margaret of Austria coming to restore to her father the contract of marriage broken by Charles VIII. We may ask why the artist has crowned the father and the daughter with an auriole, since neither one nor the other was canonized after death, and could not be so during

---

* Generally known, and at first described, as the order of the Mathurins, from their founder, John de Matha, who saw a vision—when the bishop, raising the Host, exclaimed, "Accipe Sanctum Spiritum "—of an angel clothed in white, bearing a cross on his chest of two colours, azure and scarlet, which was the prognostic of the order which he was about to institute. Being in company with a holy hermit near Meaux, they saw a stag quenching its thirst at a clear stream, and having between its horns a cross resembling that which St. John vowed to the angel when he celebrated his first mass ; he determined to build the house of his order on this spot. He went to Rome and told the Pope (Innocent III.) of his intention to dedicate his monks to the deliverance of captives ; the Pope confirmed their rule (A.D. 1107), and named the order " Of the Trinity of the redemption of captives." Matha, having founded the convent of St. Thomas at Rome, died there in the year 1214.—See "Briefve Histoire de l'Institution des Ordres Religieux." Du Fresne. Paris, 1658.

their lives? The only possible explanation is, that perhaps the artist desired to support the strange pretension of Maximilian, who caused himself to be named Pontifex Maximus, after the fashion of the Roman emperors, and absolutely wished the Pope to take him as coadjutor in the pontificate." The writer seems to forget that living persons were occasionally crowned with the nimbus. (See Didron's "Christian Iconography," page 80.)

The cut seems to represent a female undergoing the trial by fire, as she appears to be walking over (red-hot) ploughshares, the third figure possibly representing the executioner. The impossibility of such an event having taken place must be obvious, as none of the chroniclers have mentioned it. What she holds in her right hand may be, if it is meant for a trial, a piece of red-hot iron, such as was used in the Middle Ages, or it may be a box containing the marriage contract.

In addition to those gentlemen whose friendly services have been already acknowledged, the Editor has to express his gratitude to G. Voigt, J. G. Wehner, and Frederick Unger, Esqrs., especially to the first-named gentleman, for translating the archaic text of German works; and to his son, Lees Aspland, for valuable assistance.

This should have appeared as a note at page 10, but by an accident the editor omitted it.

Dr. Bryce, in alluding to Maximilian's obtaining leave from Pope Julius II. to assume the title of Imperator electus, says (page 318): "After Ferdinand, each assumed, after his German coronation, the title of Emperor Elect, and employed this in all documents issued in his name. But the word 'elect' being omitted when he was addressed by others, partly from motives of courtesy, partly because the old rules regarding the Roman coronation were forgotten, or remembered only by antiquaries, he was never called, even when formality was required, anything but Emperor." Gerard Roo (page 437), speaking of his coronation, in 1508, by the Pope's legate, has this passage : "Nö jam regem, ut hactenus, sed Romanorum Imperatorem deinceps appellandum, promulgari jubet."

THE Council of the HOLBEIN SOCIETY desire to record their deep regret at the loss of the Rev. HENRY GREEN, M.A., their first editor. He devoted his well-earned leisure, with an almost youthful enthusiasm, to the interests of the HOLBEIN SOCIETY. His scholarly mind, literary aptitude, and unusual powers of work enabled him to edit with great success the reproductions of our Society. Lovers of emblem literature are under great obligations to him for an exhaustive essay on this subject; and still more so for his volume, "Shakespeare and the Emblem-writers," which is a work of great merit.

.

Milton Keynes UK
Ingram Content Group UK Ltd.
UKHW040929180224
437992UK00003B/126